ARON BEAUREGARD'S

HALLUCINATIONS

ISBN: 9798663257107

Cover & Interior Art Copyright © 2020 Anton Rosovsky

Copyright TOC Art © 2020 Katherine Burns

Secret Art Copyright © 2020 bagasxbrojo

Edited by Laura Wilkinson

Printed in the USA

Maggot Press
Coventry, Rhode Island

WARNING

This book contains scenes and subject matter that are disgusting and disturbing, easily offended people are not the intended audience.

JOIN MY MAGGOT MAILING LIST NOW FOR EXCLUSIVE OFFERS AND UPDATES BY EMAILING
AronBeauregardHorror@gmail.com

WWW.EVILEXAMINED.COM

DEADICATION

This book is dedicated to all of my psychedelic brothers &
sisters. You know who you are, and I couldn't have been
more humbled to be terrified and enlightened beside you.
We had to go through hell to get to heaven. Our journeys
together are priceless; I wouldn't trade them for the world.
I love you all and will forever cherish our otherworldly
adventures.

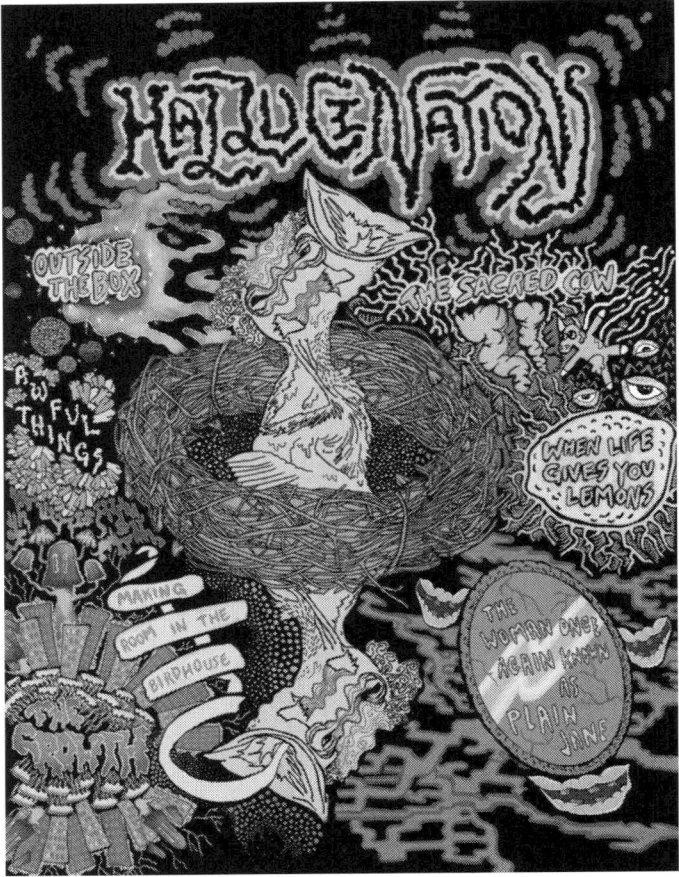

CONTENTS

ACKNOWLEDGMENTS

This book would not be possible without both my tortures and bliss coiling around each other like two slimy serpents. If you're too afraid, let my horrors explain where your mind can go at the worst of times and the euphoria it can reach at the pinnacle. It is my hope that someday you find courage as there are some things you must find a way to experience for yourself.

Some words of advice for those who choose the more audacious avenue; just hang in there. Sometimes the rollercoaster has really nice cushy seats and runs on a brand-new smooth track, other times, it's a scary, old, rickety piece of shit. Eventually, they both lead you to the same place, at least in my experience…

THE GROWTH

When the growth started, they said it was just on one man. They don't know why it started or how it evolved to be what it was, but over time what began as a simple goiter soon swelled to skyscraper-sized dimensions. An enormous all-consuming ball of sickening cysts, teeth, hair, blood, and skin.

The sphere of sinew grew by touch, bonding with everyone unfortunate enough to come into contact with it. As it expanded, it pushed down the structures around it, creating a bubbling crater of humanity smack in the middle of downtown. Apparently, our city wasn't the only place where these appalling circular flesh bags started to appear. It was all over the radio with constant coverage on every station.

You would think when people found out that the mass was absorbing whatever it encountered that they would stay away, but what's that old saying again? Oh, yes, curiosity killed the cat. In this case, it didn't kill the cat necessarily, but it did gobble it up and enslave it to become a microcosm of an endlessly capable and obscene organism. It warped them into a perverse, cruel purgatory of which there would be no finality.

Anyone who decided to set their gaze and marvel at the monstrosity became compelled to investigate it, and in investigating the veiny gristle, it seemed they had no choice but to become part of it. For unknown reasons, the thing was captivating. Its pulsating slimy casing drew them in without fail, much like the shiny gold watch swinging beneath the hypnotist's hand.

When I heard about the thousands that had flocked to witness the behemoth eyesore, popcorn ready only to never return, I became deeply concerned. The voices on the radio sounded more concerned too. They talked about the army troops that were sent in to obliterate the gore sack. How platoon after platoon set their rifles aside and walked into it with open arms. They talked about how the airplanes that came to drop bombs on it wound up inside it. They'd adopted the tactics of the enemy we were currently at war with overseas; they'd become strange spur-of-the-moment kamikazes.

Thankfully, I was cautious in the beginning. Maybe it was my cowardice that kept me alive. I wanted to see the thing just as much as the rest but the grave consequences made it glaringly obvious that I should wait for more information. I set out to the store having decided that I would wait it out. Running wouldn't help, the broadcasts had made it clear that these things were appearing randomly all across the country now.

With the rapid spread fresh in mind, I stopped at the hardware supply to acquire some heavy chain and shackles. I carefully plotted my route around all the areas that the reports indicated the strange mass could be observed. Before I headed back home, I stopped at the market and stocked up on a few months' worth of non-perishables.

The people at the grocery store were terrified, but business had to continue. Everyone was just extra conscious about the growth and staying clear of it. The food supply was dwindling; the truckers were dropping like flies. One wrong turn on their route and they were driving their wide-loads straight into the belly of the abomination. Others just retired out of the pure terror and anxiety derived from the current situation. They were probably just like me, stocking up and preparing to wait out the strangeness. The few brave souls that were still on the road were the real heroes; they were keeping the shelves from going entirely barren.

When I returned home, I decided the safest thing I could do would be to shackle myself to the bed and keep the food and radio nearby. The chain was long enough to allow me to get around the apartment, just not outside of it. It was a vigilant precaution but far from overkill. Now all that was left to do was wait.

***

Weeks went by and still, no one had figured out how to combat the fucking thing. Where were the scientists? Shouldn't these guys be able to crack this by now or had they all become part of it? My outlook was growing grim just as rapidly as the ghoulish satchel inflated. With each passing day, the atmosphere became more frightening. I was running out of supplies and couldn't decide if another potentially lethal trip to the store was feasible. Eventually, it was going to have to happen, but I'd rather wait and wonder then venture out into the absurd uncertainty.

***

I only had about another weeks' worth of rations left until I was going to have to make a move. The lone man left on the radio seemed to be growing madder by the day. All of a sudden, he'd changed his tune. His focus has shifted and he now was telling everyone that they should try not to think about it. He claimed that they were discovering now just merely seeing it in your mind could cause people to be attracted to it.

How is that even possible? Rendering a visual of something you've never seen before can trigger some kind of a metaphysical magnetic pull? How is this reality?

The whole concept was unquestionably insane. The bizarre premise that this thing of unknown origin was swallowing up the world was like nothing that mankind had ever heard. I mean how could you not think about it? Had we awakened it or had we created it? Part of me felt that it couldn't even be real. Was it all just some mass mirage? Some strange conspiracy?

***

I couldn't stop thinking about the fucking thing no matter how hard I tried. Ever since that bastard on the radio suggested we try not to, it felt like I was in constant competition. I'd exhausted myself like a hamster running on a wheel with attempt after attempt. I tried to think of other events, memories, or even people I'd screwed; anything to keep my mind off it.

The man on the radio had stopped talking a couple of days ago. Part of me wondered if he had thought about the growth a little too much himself. Maybe I should unlock my shackle and go to the store to get more food? Looking at the rations I realized that I still had another few days of food covered…

I didn't know what to think, had I been tricking myself? Was I really wanting to unlock my chain to re-up on supplies or was that just what I was convincing myself the reason was? Would I just go running like a madman off into the blubbery ball as soon as the cold steel unlocked?

The fact that I was asking those questions proved that I couldn't be trusted. Now I wanted more than anything to open the lock, then I could have a peek at what all the fuss was about. NO! FUCK! I would go get food I mean! I would not have a peek at the growth; I would just get the supplies that I required in order to survive the upcoming weeks.

The way I was thinking wasn't safe. I made a rash decision and picked the tiny key off my nightstand, raised my glass of water, and chugged it down in a single gulp. As the steel made its way down my throat, I felt relief in my mind for the first time in weeks.

Now I couldn't leave for another day or so at least, not until I had enough time for the key to work its way through my intestines before I shit it out. That would give me plenty of time to forget about the gigantic growth that everyone had been talking about. The colossal bulb of entrancing humanity... The gore cluster of doom... The blood-bag of downtown...

***

I awoke standing over the kitchen sink, the knife was already in my hand and poking into my abdomen. Maybe it was the pain that had brought me back. I was shocked to see what was unfolding; I had been regulated to full-on spectator mode as desires and irreversible cravings unfamiliar to me had begun to pilot all of my movements.

My free hand was saturated in the warm dark red that spewed out from the gaping hole that I was fishing around in. It wasn't until I felt my fingers squeeze my stomach that I realized what was happening. As I pulled out my precious food storage compartment, my knife-wielding extremity promptly slit it open.

I ripped it apart like a savage that felt nothing but an absolute and malicious motivation to unveil the organ's contents. I pushed some of the undigested, mushy oats out that I had eaten before bed and uncovered the small slimy key. I dropped both the knife and my stomach then freed my ankle at once. I didn't bother to put my stomach and entrails that were spraying out like silly string back inside my torso. I just stormed off and dragged them behind me. I had something far more important to see than my body become whole again.

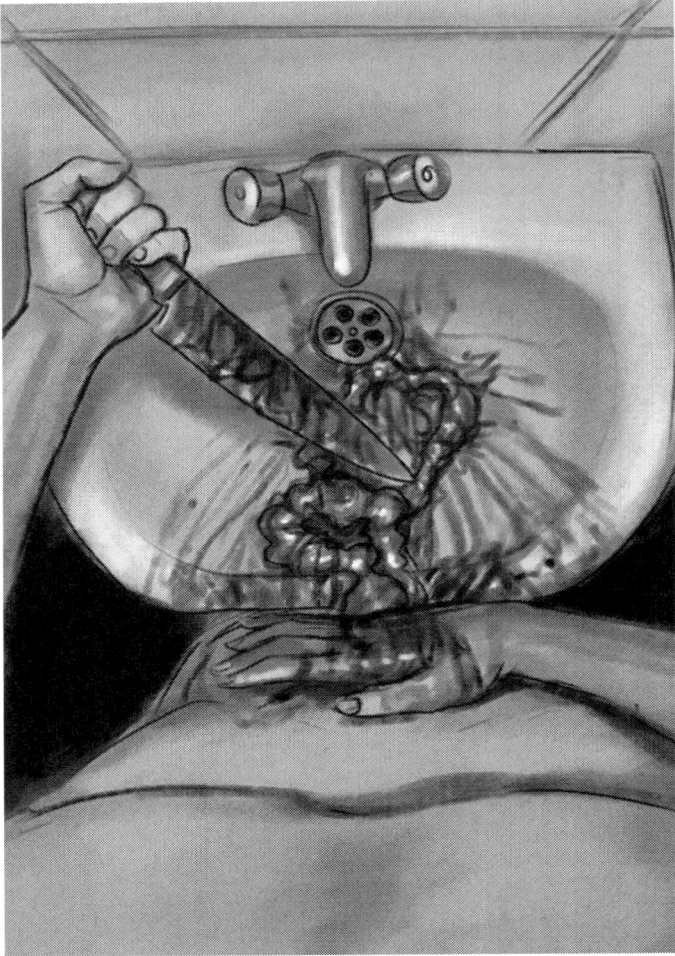

When I made it downtown, my guts had picked up some glass and other garbage that littered the city. It wasn't long before I finally appeared in front of it. The hot oily pink meat opened its gates for me like I was a first-class citizen. As I stepped in closer, I noticed that many others were still making their way toward the growth. In some inexplicable way, it felt beautiful.

Maybe it was because I had no choice and my path was now definite but I felt an incredible amount of relief again. It was different than the variety I felt in the apartment. This was an all-encompassing liberation. As I penetrated the growth the warm meat and inelastic bones fondled every inch of my body. I felt at home. While the teeth chattered and bit into my skin, away went all my complications. As the hair and eyeballs massaged my limbs, I giggled with glee.

Why had I been so scared? It was nothing to be afraid of, it never had been…

Suddenly, my vision grew distorted and the trembling pink walls parted again. This time, I saw a blinding light; one that overpowered my vision until it slowly adjusted. As I was pulled out the slit of light, I felt suffocated. My ankle where the shackle once was now felt tremendous pressure. As I left the walls of the growth's warm pink meat, I felt like my equilibrium had been thrown off; I was upside down.

When my eyes came back into focus, and the richer details became more evident, I could see that the pressure on my joint was being generated from a mammoth blood-stained green glove that was clamped around it. Additionally, my leg now looked entirely different; it was shrunken, fragile, and fresh. My toes were no bigger than tiny kernels of corn...

As I dangled in the air helplessly, I was suddenly struck with a firm slap on the ass. The power and sting of the strike sent me screeching into a fit. Tears rained in reverse down the top of my head and fell to the sterile-looking floor. The hand dropped me down into the skin of a thick, fatigued, and equally teary-eyed woman.

The warmth and love I felt from her were like the sun rising a thousand times. Her face was filled with a harmony that she fed into me. I didn't know how long it would take to get back to the end again but the beginning was more stunning than anything I'd ever experienced. I just hoped that this time, I'd be able to remember it.

WHEN LIFE GIVES YOU LEMONS

"What, are you scared or something? I never thought I'd see the day when Jake Palmer turned down a drug," Byron crooned as he headed over to the minibar and set himself up with another Kennedy cocktail.

Sasha and Phoebe looked equally perplexed; out of the entire lot of them, Jake was the staunchest advocate for fueling the group's continuous debauchery. He'd experimented with more drugs than the FDA but there was a strong hesitation within him that day.

"Have you had it before?" Jake asked.

"What does it matter to you? This is some next-level shit right here, supposedly it makes DMT look like fucking roses."

"I don't know, I got a weird feeling…"

"Honey, what's wrong? Are you alright?" Phoebe seemed more concerned than confused.

"Feeling? Since when do you feel? Do you have any idea how difficult it is to land this shit? I put my ass on the line and bend over backwards to make this happen and now you're bailing? What the fuck, Jake?" Byron wasn't letting him off easily.

"I'm not bailing, but why can't we just do it once we get to the resort?"

"Because there is no time better to blast off than when you're already twenty-thousand feet in the air."

"Baby, I promise I won't let anything happen to you, okay?" Phoebe massaged the top of his hand and thigh.

Jake looked out the oval window just past the luxury leather sofa that Sasha was seated on. The clouds looked heavenly with the warm mandarin sun slipping through from the top. While the visuals helped to comfort him, the inexplicable sensation that gnawed at his guts was still there.

Byron didn't mind serving up anyone who needed convincing. The silver-tongued charlatan reseated himself beside his sexy wife and swallowed nearly half his drink before breaking the awkward silence.

"Listen, buddy, the facts are that we've got another sixteen hours to Bali. I'm sorry to burst your bubble but I really don't think long islands, gin rummy, and good old-fashioned chit-chat with you and the ladies is gonna cut it for me. We all got onto my plane with the same agenda. Everyone is on board with this except you; the one guy who should be fuckin' automatic. Don't ruin this trip for us." His tone was no longer warm and fuzzy, it was cold and manipulative.

"You *really* want me to jump off this fuckin' plane, don't you?"

Byron smiled, "You know it."

"Alright, have it your way," Jake finally conceded.

"Now that's what I'm talking about! Yes!"

The loud announcement speaker behind the four of them crackled and a smooth voice began to speak, "Mr. Maxwell, please be advised we might have a little patch of turbulence approaching shortly."

"Perfect timing, we better get these things in now," Byron said while rising to his heels.

"In… What do you mean in?" Phoebe inquired.

He ignored her and stepped into the bathroom at the rear of the plane, closing the door behind him.

"You have to stick them up your ass," Sasha replied casually.

Phoebe looked to Jake to gauge his outrage but he was just staring out the window again. "That seems like a lot of work… And it's disgusting."

"Sweetie, please, your peacocking is priceless but we all know your ass has seen more inanimate objects than an antique mall. It's like you forget sometimes that we're the ones you share your darkness with; we're the ones you get fucked up with, remember?"

Phoebe blushed and giggled as she was swamped with particles of her more shameful remembrances. She wasn't the brainiest broad but she had a refreshing consideration and tolerance about her. They needed to have someone of her character weaved into their cynical assemblage. If not as the moral mediator for every time they went too far, then just for sheer variability purposes. Misery needs company.

"Plus, when you take it up the ass, you feel it right away. We're trying to do the right thing on this flight, are we not?" Sasha lit a joint while already in the clouds, something that only filthy rich pricks like themselves could check off their bucket list. "Jake, you've got me really curious about you today. I just have to know… You literally took PCP before your own mother's funeral… I'm not going to rehash the details but, I mean, if you can go that fucking far, why the hesitation today over a measly plane ride?"

"I told you why—I have a bad feeling. You know, like when your guts feel like they just went skydiving. That's what I feel. Like my mind told my body what was about to go down. Like it was sending me a signal."

"That sounds scary, baby," Phoebe interjected.

He looked at her, oozing genuine concern, then back to Sasha who only sought to answer entertaining inquires. "But I didn't want to ruin your husband's precious fucking plane ride, so I'm going against my nagging instincts so he doesn't have a sixteen-hour hissy fit."

"That kind of you," Sasha said, passing the joint.

"I mean, we're going to Bali to tool around for a

month. Attend every party and bang out every drug imaginable, but he's got his panties in a bunch over a flight? We're all ungrateful… And sometimes it's just sickening really. Maybe that's the true root of my apprehension."

Sasha raised her shellacked black-licorice nails in front of her skin-tugging fake breasts. They presented a canyon of cleavage as the backdrop for her slow clap. "Bravo, Jake. It only took you, what?" she looked at her forearm like there was a wrist-watch there, "thirty-six summers to figure that out? I'm pretty sure you figured it out a long time before that and just didn't give a good fuck. We were born into this life; we didn't choose it. Am I supposed to be *grateful* that my esophagus is deteriorating because I'm forced to maintain this figure?" she asked, gesturing toward her torso. "Should I be *grateful* that I've seen the world and now there's nothing left but depression? Should I be *grateful* that I need to balance my uppers and downers every day like a fucking swimming pool to keep the razor away from my wrist? People think this is all blessings, but you know just as well as I do that the water is never clear. It's a murky jaded swamp-full of leeches."

Before Jake could respond, Byron burst out of the bathroom. "I finally got it, took a little work but it's in there…" he slurred staggering back to the sofa. He set the chrome pillbox down on the coffee table. The top of the fine tin bubbled outward with an ominous mold in the outline of a particularly upsetting interpretation of Lucifer. It was a curiously-detailed closeup of his multihorned head, brandishing tickled fangs while dragging fat snakes from the depths of his eye cavities. The exaggerated features made Jake uncomfortable.

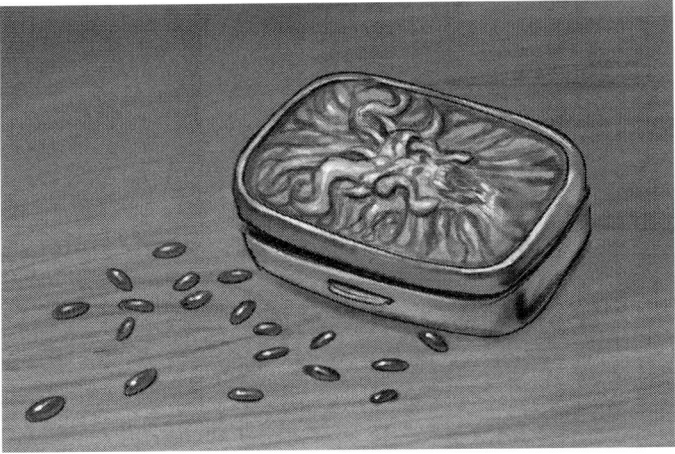

Byron pulled open the tin to reveal a slew of clear gel caps that contained a portentous ruby filling. "Here it is, everybody grab one."

Phoebe held one the long way up to the light cutting in through the window. The spellbinding substance slithered around in the contained space between her thumb and trigger-finger. "What's this called again?" she asked now with a hint of the jitters.

The life looked like it had already drained out from Byron's buttery eyeballs as he whispered, "Limbo."

"Why's that?" Phoebe asked naively as if there should be a distinct correlation to the effects of every drug and its name.

"Trust me, you'll find out soon enough."

Something about his snooty answer didn't sit well with her but it also didn't come close to stopping her from being the first one into the bathroom to push the pill up her rectum.

One by one, they continued to file in until they were all back where they'd started, but not really... The limbo had dissolved and quickly absorbed into their submissive tissues. What was normally strictly an exit (for most of them anyway) had now become an entrance for entrancement; a gaping doorway toward welcomed delusion.

The visuals were indescribable. They were dripping all over the gaudy fixtures they'd found comfort in previously. One thing that they were all aware of from past experience was that comfort was not something afforded while transcending dimensions. They were all peeling back their many layers of deceit. As the light shined and illuminated them, they were being ripped apart molecule by molecule.

To Byron, suddenly the bar looked more like a cave. He might be required to go spelunking the next time he needed a refill. For the first time, the drink didn't seem all that important anymore. His glass fell down onto the Valencia gray carpet, leaving a stain on both the floor and his brain that would be difficult to forget.

To Sasha, her friends looked stretched past the limits of the universe but still whole. Their heads seemed to be levitating high above them to absurd giraffe-like altitudes. They were ugly but they were themselves. She couldn't help but feel a morbid Frankenstein-like feeling gripping her as the jelly inside her implants shuddered above her ribcage.

To Phoebe, her eyelids needed to stay closed. The things she saw in her friends and lover couldn't be the truth but her spiritual clarification was definitive. Their hellish drooling frowns and hemorrhaging sockets were regurgitating all of their blackened sins. The river of molten ills seemed limitless and the more she saw, the more offended she grew. She decided to shift the course of her hallucinations by closing her eyes. *Why am I with them?* she wondered before pushing her rotten acquaintances out of sight and mind.

That was a question to reflect on after the trip. She was now permitted to drip through the mega cosmos of blithe benevolence that her inner being fueled. The freedom was relieving as the profound bulk of her sick companions' misdeeds was finally relinquished. She had been freed from her human shackles and left to the fluttering kaleidoscope of four-dimensional insignias.

To Jake, it was all where it had started; right in the window. He'd found the rabbit hole; the window fell outward and snaked off, forming a transparent tubular tunnel. The clear cylindrical shaft beckoned him to climb inside and explore like a child at the McDonald's Play Place. The clouds around the winding see-through maze were white no more—they were gloomy and green like the flesh of the Wicked Witch of the West.

The more he stared at them, the more he realized that they weren't clouds at all. They were clusters of drippy warts; warts of the midnight toxic variety. Their bumpy roundness ballooned outward, tearing at the seams of the bunches as they suffocated and squirmed through the labyrinth of curious plumbing. As the swelling caused more of the emerald juice to rain down, a voice in his head grew in volume. *You must find what you've come for, you must go inside now…*

The voice left behind a deceitful first impression. It couldn't be trusted. Internally, he knew that he needed to move away from the bulbous, soaring epidermis and strange tubes. His head slowly rotated around while his spine clicked internally with each peg that turned. A mysterious sensation surrounded his vertebrae like someone had poured a fizzing soda pop inside him. The rotation defied any human options. Jake's throat flesh pruned and it became harder for him to breathe, but the difficulty was worth what lingered out the window aligned to his back.

The black craft blocked out the entire sky for as far as his eyes could see. His chest thrashed relentlessly as he scanned the smooth, wet, onyx outline. The wide platform extended for miles, floating threateningly while keeping a parallel pace with the plane.

Two gigantic figures that were slender and spikey stepped to the edge of the platform. They wavered in the force of the air but didn't fight the winds, instead their bodies conformed to the conditions. They looked like unnerving versions of the inflatable dancing men.

The pilot's voice interjected concern, "Do you see that outside? Jesus, Joseph, Mary… What in the fuck is that thing?! I'm going to try and pull away from it. Mr. Maxwell, I need everyone to take their seats, NOW!" His voice sounded like it was traveling out to the group in waves.

No one seemed capable of reacting; they were all trapped in limbo.

Jake remained mesmerized by the figures which were further highlighted by the birch flashes that filled the select slices of skyline that hadn't been blocked out behind them. As they swayed back and forth, Jake wondered if their environment was controlling them or if their ability to adapt in truth meant they were the ones in control…

The flight all of a sudden sharply surpassed being just shaky. The course had been mildly turbulent since the pilot had made his announcement, but their path had rapidly grown bumpier. *Does it have to do with those curious "men" watching on outside? Are they a part of it?* Jake wondered.

Unexpectedly, wide blinding beams of light made their way into the cabin. Jake's cranium screwed itself tighter as his head turned to observe the laser-like shots that were now projected onto his friends. Their bodies were illuminated magnificently by the flickers, like they had been surrounded with walking x-rays.

Their bones looked like they were comprised of an abnormal gooey matter as they levitated off the rug, the secret strings which controlled them becoming visible. They were slaves to the fishing wire; the unusual men had used their unfamiliar tools to unveil it. As the cords were tugged harder, they danced more violently, executing hyper bends and inhuman contortion. They were at the mercy of the unusual men.

As they moved at illogical speed, the plane began to tremor as if an earthquake had found its way on board. The neon skeletons that were Jake's friends overlapped with streaks of color that looked like they came from a drunken rage-filled painter. As his contaminated dome continued on a swivel, watching them trace and retrace their pattern was mind-numbing.

High-pitch shrieks began to worm their way in from the black craft still riding alongside the plane outside. The flashes and beams were more intense than any Fourth of July spectacle; a seizure-worthy light show. It was chaos as the dark craft smashed into the side of the plane, knocking all four of them to the floor.

The plane speaker cracked with the pilot's voice again. "Everyone get in your fucking seats now! It's, it's running us down! I can't, I can't get the nose up, oh God, we're going down!" His voice had now morphed into a mix of southern twang and demonic.

Something about this second announcement had a deeper impact. Jake somehow found his legs while his head gradually turned like a ballerina in a music box. It made it difficult to find his way to the eight, typically unused, traditional airplane chairs. These had belts and buckles that could keep you fixed.

By the time he'd gotten there, and his vision lined up correctly, he found that Byron and Sasha had already buckled down, but his sweet tender Phoebe was still sprawled out on the leather with her eyes sealed shut. As the plane continued its nosedive, gravity was angling them toward the cockpit. Phoebe needed to join them fast or else she wouldn't have a chance of survival.

"Honey, come here! Take a seat, come quickly!" he screamed like it was his last words to her. It was like he was calling out to a tired old ghost; she remained in position unwaveringly with her eyes closed tight.

"I'm going to see the stars now, baby. I'm ready, I've never been more ready."

"Phoebe! You have to come now!" Jake tried to get out of his seat but Byron fastened his belt. They had teetered too far to take a walk.

The plane continued its plunge while Phoebe slid off the couch away from them. "The stars... They're so beautiful." Jake watched the letters leave her mouth as her body then crashed violently into the cockpit door. The sickening crack of her frame hitting it was the last noise they heard coming from her.

Jake looked out the window at the flashing cyclone of psychedelic madness. The black platform was just a short distance away still and those sinister beings had now solidified their form. They were no longer waving in the breakneck breeze; they were standing tall with their darkness shining. The slender shadows snuffed out all sight as they moved in.

Instantaneously, it was like three black garbage bags had been wrapped around each of their heads. They struggled in their chairs as their ears popped and they got closer to the Earth's surface. The sound of metal colliding with water assaulted their ears as they all simultaneously lost consciousness.

***

When Jake awoke, he first felt the soft sensation of tiny granular sand against his sweaty face and bare hands. The sweat, blood, and salty taste in his mouth were as uncomfortable as the scorching sun rays that cooked him inside his Brooks Brothers Milano athletic fit blazer. He used his arms to push himself up from the face-down pose and unbuttoned the overpriced jacket.

As he steadily regained his bearings and examined his surroundings, he noticed the crumpled plane wreck still smoking behind him. He was sitting in beach sand with a few floatation devices in his circumference. The airplane was demolished and partially submerged in the ocean water but somehow, it was just a short swim away from land.

He took another glance around him and confirmed that there was no one to be seen. Without hesitation, he made his way into the choppy waters. He swam with the vigor and passion of an eager child heading downstairs on Christmas morning; as fast as humanly possible.

As Jake pulled himself onto the broken wing of the craft, he readied his body to take a leap. He landed midsection first onto the lip of the plane exit. He pulled up and prepared for the absolute worst as he stepped into the cabin once again.

He looked left first where they had all originally been seated and saw utter destruction. The back of the aircraft had been blown out entirely and he could see the sun off in the distance. Nearly everything that was inside had been gutted. All that remained were the seats that they'd last buckled themselves into before impact and some cabinets that normally held snacks and party favors. Sadly, the fixtures were ajar and bare.

His brain had been aching the entire time as he tried to comprehend what was real. *Am I still in limbo?* There was no true way to be sure at the moment. Reality and wherever he had ventured to during the horrific air cruise were two entirely different things. Some of the walls and details upon up-close inspection appeared to be moving; he was in the process of coming down.

It wasn't relentless and as much of an insane mess as before, but it was still there. *How long have I been out for?* Jake pulled himself out of his selfish thoughts and back to why he'd returned to the plane; Phoebe.

Whether it was real or not, he recalled her parting words to him and that her body had been slung toward the cockpit. He did a one-eighty and came face to face with her again, just not the way that he'd hoped.

The first thing he saw was her stomach and the spider tattoo that she had near her hip. She was bent in half like a full-body folding beach chair which had been collapsed into itself twice. Her skin had been split and her essence and organs had found light. She looked like a human sandwich being projected through a funhouse mirror. Her state was so dreadful that looking her in the eye one final time to say goodbye wasn't an option.

He took a few moments that were comprised of frenetic crying and apologies before finally regaining composure. She was a kind and tender woman and it was his fault that she was on the flight in the first place. While he knew she wasn't exactly the type of woman he pictured himself beside five years from then, he had love for her. Phoebe had a gentle and pure soul. She deserved better than him and his crude comrades to be the last thing in her sights.

The guilt felt far heftier than poor Phoebe's petite mangled carcass as he dragged it from the doorway of the cockpit. Things had taken a turn for the worse, he needed to start thinking about what the fuck his next step was. He was starting to think about himself again and snapping into survival mode.

Jake knew he needed to see if the pilot was in any better condition than his lover. The plane was torn to shit but maybe the pilot was alive, maybe he could still call for help…

He banged on the door with his fist, "Hey, buddy, can you hear me in there? Are you okay?"

No response or sounds made their way back.

Jake stepped away, he noticed that the door was discombobulated already. One good shot would get him inside. He charged forward, lowering the shoulder, and blew it open with ease. What was on the other side was not what he'd hoped.

There had clearly been a raging fire inside that the below water wasn't quite tall enough to extinguish. The pilot sat strapped into his chair, still wearing the charred remnants of his stupid fucking hat and sporting a customer service-friendly smile. It wasn't because he was filled with joy though, it was because he had burned down to blackened bones and his face had gone up in smoke.

Jake was shocked and mortified at first but again, his own personal wellbeing was pushing him to remove any emotion from his thoughts. He was less connected to the pilot so that made things a little easier. "I guess smiling is the only option for you now…" he remarked, focusing on the gum-less teeth. He looked down at the frayed belt. "Fuck, must've been dead or unconscious while he burned alive."

He took his gaze away from the gruesome corpse and focused on the control dashboard. "Shit," he mumbled defeatedly, examining the long-melted panel of shifters, cracked gauges, and joysticks. Part of him questioned if the drugs were making him see the oozing mechanics but he felt them with his hands and confirmed that it was no joke—he was fucked.

***

After coming up empty on any potentially useful items while sifting through the wreckage, Jake solemnly made his way back to the shore. He had no idea where they'd landed but he knew that he would need to explore immediately and find out if anyone else was nearby. *Where the fuck are Bryon and Sasha? They aren't on the plane, so where the hell could they have gone?*

He decided to stick to the shoreline, surely he could locate a boat preparing to exit or enter the land quickly. Everything he passed all kind of looked the same; exotic palm trees, soft sand, and random brush were the only things in sight. After about forty or so minutes of walking in the daunting heat, finally he saw it—the crashed airplane. It was clear now that he was on an island and it was a rather small one…

It was apparent that no one was within thousands of miles of where the plane went down. Jake knew there was nothing left for him at the shoreline except dehydration and heatstroke. He needed to head into the trees and brush because there was simply no other alternative.

As he stepped into the exotic vegetation, a myriad of ramblings raced in his mind: *I can't drink seawater, it drives you mad and kills you. I'll need food soon… I'm beginning to feel feeble. Maybe there are animals on the island? Maybe there is some kind of berries or pineapples? Coconuts have water inside, there has to be something here… Did Sasha and Byron drown or did they leave to try and find food and water? If they're here I need to find them.*

The words continued to run through his mind over and over as his eyes cut around the large leafy plants obstructing his view. He trekked on straight ahead, searching for energy to muster and boost him forward. There didn't seem to be much variety in the plant life on the island; that didn't bode well in his mind.

Exhaustion was sinking its teeth into his legs. Jake's run to the plane around the edges of the island, and attempt to penetrate its center had taken a parasitic toll on him. His energy had dwindled, he couldn't recall the last time he had a nibble of nourishment or drink of water. *How much further can I go? Gotta keep pushing…*

As doubt began to mar his judgment, suddenly, he heard a rustling just a short distance away. Layered over the moving leaves, the sounds of voices projected toward him. Jake pushed forward with everything he had left and was able to stumble through the green wall of vegetation and spill into a small circular clearing.

Within the boatload of seaside powder laid out in the open space, he saw both his fellow companions, Byron and Sasha. They were seated under the shade of an orchard of fully bloomed fruit trees. It was a miracle! By the random power of fate itself, they had somehow been stranded on an island where they still had access to a food source! The vigorous and sturdy trees were aplenty with… Lemons?

"I thought you guys were dead," Jake spoke, his words shocking them like electricity from behind.

"Jake?" Byron removed the partially torn-apart

lemon from his mouth. He couldn't believe it was him. "Thought you were dead."

"More like you left me for dead. You don't have to be a doctor to find a heartbeat."

"We were gonna check on you, we just wanted to look for food and drinkable water first," Sasha replied.

"Yeah, cuz that makes sense, leaving me face down in the sand to fuckin' roast in this hundred-degree weather. I guess it was too much to ask you to drag me under a palm tree?"

"No, we were—"

Jake didn't allow Sasha to further her nonsense, "Or did you just not give a fuck?"

"Forgive me, I was just a little bit off considering I'd just been in a fucking plane crash. You should be happy we pulled your heavy ass out of that wreck back there!" Byron rebutted.

"You weren't too off to sniff out the one goddamn area on the whole island with food though, were you? Just save it, Byron, you were never my friend, you were just another face to get laced with. Go spew your usual bullshit to someone else because it's obvious that taking two minutes of your time to save my life just didn't rank up there in your priorities, did it?"

"Just calm down both of you! We can't waste the little energy we have arguing. If we're gonna live, we need to be smart," Sasha explained.

Their connected death-stare didn't budge but their argument died out. As much as Jake didn't want to admit it, she was right. He was castaway on a strange island in the middle of nowhere with two people who only thought about themselves. He would need to be careful about how he spent his time and fuel, and he would have to monitor the situation very shrewdly.

"So, lemons? That's all we have then?" Jake had a great deal of disbelief to offer.

"We searched every inch of this hellhole, I mean, I'm no survivalist, but I think I have a general idea of what would be edible. Everything else is just palm trees, dirt, and bushes," Sasha explained.

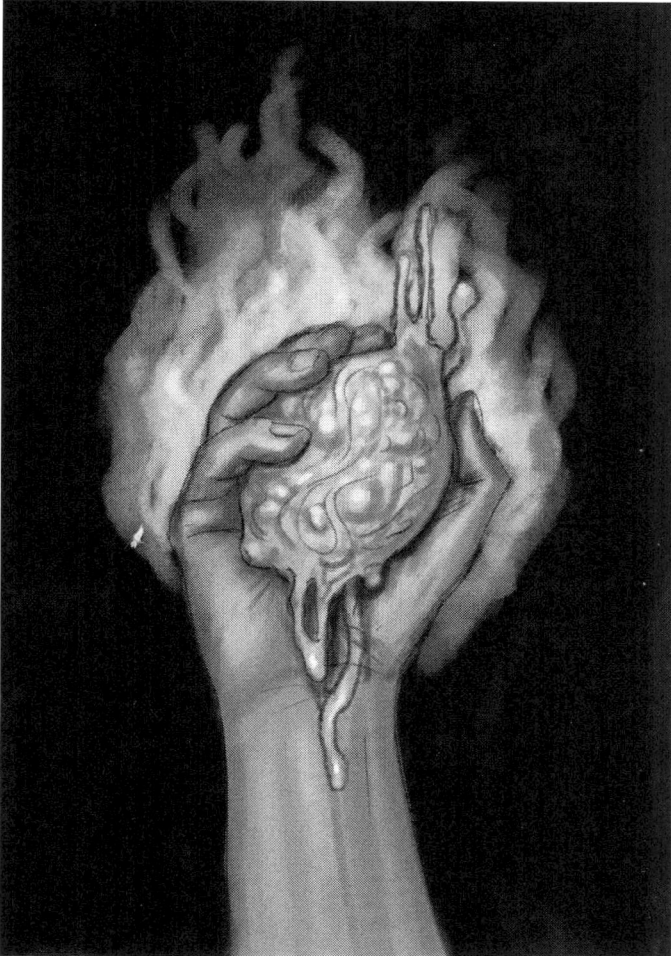

"Fuck," Jake mumbled.

"This fruit seems like the only thing that would give us any sort of nutrients," Sasha continued.

"Did you guys go back on the plane?" Jake asked.

"Yes… And I'm sorry. I'm terribly sorry to have to tell you this, but Phoebe is… Phoebe's dead, Jake." She tried to appear emotional, even sprinkling a little voice crack as she spoke, but Jake knew it was all a show.

"And there was no food or water left on the plane? Not even some crackers or something?"

"Nothing, unfortunately…"

"That's interesting because I went back onto the plane myself and the snack cabinets were still intact, just open and empty."

"Well, the crash must have sent it seaworthy, Jake, I don't know what you want us to tell you. We didn't steal the fucking crackers," Byron replied.

Jake thought to himself for a minute looking up at the round orange sun. "Did you see them?"

"See who?" Byron began sucking on the lemon again with a grimace.

"The strange men. They were standing on the edge of that aircraft outside the window of the plane. They were watching us before we crashed…"

"You were in limbo, Jake, what you were seeing wasn't reality."

"Was the pilot in limbo too? I heard him mention it, you heard him mention it."

"Was that the pilot or was that just one of the other hundred or so other voices talking in your head while you were in limbo? Because I didn't hear shit aside from some demons telling me to do some incredibly horrible things…"

Jake rushed at Byron and slammed him against the

30

trunk of a lemon tree. A handful of the ripened fruit detached and landed in the sand. "I told you I had a bad fucking feeling about this trip, didn't I! I told you I didn't want to do it! Now, Phoebe's dead! Now we're all fucking dead because you had to get your way!"

"Fuck you, pretty boy, whether you wanna believe it or not, that little brain of yours made the choice that ultimately got you here. I didn't put that pill in your ass, you did! The plane was going down whether we tripped or not! What's done is done!"

"I was going to save her!"

"You were reaching out to the reaper! You'd be a broken pile of meat just like her if I didn't buckle you in! I had no choice, and the fact that you're guilt-tripping me for saving your life is even more ludicrous than blaming me for a freak fucking plane crash!"

"Guys! Enough! Enough!" Sasha bulled her way between them, creating some much-needed separation.

Jake walked away from them and stood under a tree a few yards away, leaning against it. Byron snatched some of the displaced fruit, holding it in his arms like they were a prized possession.

"We gotta stop focusing on before and move onto what's next. If we don't then we're all gonna be dead real soon." Sasha plucked one of the lemons that Byron left on the ground.

"We've gotta think… I'm probably not particularly useful in a situation like this but I didn't get this figure by *not* counting calories. These lemons… They can't have more than fifty or sixty calories each, which isn't shit really. The one thing on our side is that there's a lot of them. But I can't imagine, even if we ate the peels with it, we'd get by more than a few weeks on these alone."

"You ever stop and think why, on an island in the middle of fucking nowhere, there's an orchard of lemon trees?" Jake's words were seasoned with anger and sarcasm.

"What? How is that strange?" Byron replied.

"Because it's not a tropical fucking tree you idiot! Why is there not one single animal here? I haven't even encountered so much as a bug since we washed up and you don't find that the least bit odd?"

"I can appreciate your curiosity but answering those questions doesn't take us a step closer to survival. I'm exclusively interested in staying alive right now. For the first time ever, I'm a Bee Gee's gal, Jake, what about you?" Sasha waited for his response but it never came.

She took his silence as compliance and reengaged the prior topic. "So, like I was saying, we probably need to pick all the ripe ones now, see how many we have, and ration those out so we don't leave ourselves empty-handed. Then, at the beginning of each day, we can see if any others are ready to pick. Does that sound reasonable?"

Byron nodded and Jake just stared into the ground.

"I'm thinking we can try to use some of these leaves to start a fire too, keeping it running all day is our best bet at being rescued. And maybe we can gather some wood together and write help in giant letters in this clearing. If we were on this flight route, that means eventually someone else will pass overhead. We just have to hope that it's before we run out of… Lemons." She laid out some large leaves, "Here, we can keep the fruit on these in the shade and cover it, so the sun doesn't damage or cause them to spoil too soon."

Jake looked on menacingly as Byron set his haul down and turned back to the cluster of trees. He joined

Sasha and started ripping down more of the sour yellow fruit. He looked at the glowing golden exterior and mumbled, "Of all the fucking fruits…"

***

After a week of burning fires and keeping their eyes peeled, they came up empty. Jake, in particular, looked to be in bad shape. He didn't look himself; his normally athletic physique had taken a disturbing turn. The muscle had melted off and his protruding bones highlighted the grave issues at hand.

Byron and Sasha both looked stringier then before but nothing close to Jake's alarming transition. They sat in silence in an attempt to further conserve their energy. While Jake moaned and tears welled in his sunken eye sockets, all they could do was watch and listen to his suffering.

They noticed he'd begun speaking to God often, begging him to take his life. Jake clawed at his gut while he writhed in agony and sweat squeezed through his pores. The acidic citrus pooling in his guts felt like it was constantly eating away at his insides.

He was consuming close to ten lemons a day to try and keep himself hydrated and as healthy as he could considering the situation. Even after ingesting as much as he'd forced down, Jake still hadn't been able to stand up for days. As his body quaked with malnourishment and its own passive rejection of the lemons, he continued the torturous chore of extracting what little nutrients could be gained from the bitter fruit.

Each bite put a tart tingle on his tongue that left him on the verge of vomit. He gagged in front of Byron and Sasha, as his cheeks distended outward. Jake placed the back of his hand against his lips firmly as his facial skin sacks filled with partially digested peels and the lemon's nauseating extract. His throat and nasal cavity were set ablaze as he forced the burning concoction back down.

Byron and Sasha could do little to help him other than continuing to burn leaves and weave a smoke signal upward into the cobalt sky. While they had their ill effects, there were still plenty of lemons. To their astonishment, after they had picked and stored all the remaining fruit by mid-week, somehow the trees had miraculously rebloomed…

***

When Jake woke up, he was trying to scream but the blood from his belly ulcers intertwined with the juices from his acid reflux, made that impossible. He gurgled like a child drowning in shallow water as he squirmed on his back and his regurgitation launched upward into his nose and pupils.

As the fiery sensation spread across his entire face, it also traveled down to his asshole. The sour liquid and substance that were fortunate enough to make it into his bowels were leaving him like they were late for something. The brown ooze seared his sphincter tissue, it was more than irritation; it was a raging inferno that felt like it was disintegrating his anal ring.

His underwear had browned faster than fried hash; his entire essence escaped him. Somehow, he found the strength to roll around. It was a futile misinformed display as if his brain had gotten remedies confused. He wasn't literally "stop drop and roll" on fire, but he was burning alive. As he rolled in his liquified puke and shit, he finally let out a heartbreaking wail of horror.

The disturbing episode carried on as he slowly guided his confused mind down the dark railroad of doom. Jake's pathetic and stringy limbs convulsed violently as a plethora of fluids emitted one final surge from his famished decimated body just before it quit on him entirely.

***

The next morning, Byron and Sasha dragged Jake's body out by the water. They pulled it through the salty seafoam and washed all the blood, shit, and vomit off of him. Then they dragged him back to the campsite.

"I'm starving," Byron complained.

"We're almost there," Sasha reassured him.

They laid Jake's sad, distorted frame out in the shade beside the mountain of lemons which they'd previously harvested. Together, they covered his body in long green leaves. Once the task was finished, they retreated together into a meticulously built cove just a short distance away. The piles of plant life appeared normal enough, but when you pushed it aside, there was a small hidden space that was easy to overlook.

As they sat down beside each other, Sasha looked at him. "Thank God he's finally dead."

"Yep, looks like the son of a bitch got his wish," Byron replied, reaching into a backpack and extracting some crackers and beef jerky.

"I was getting tired of eating at midnight on eggshells, waiting for that cocksucker to wake up and wonder where we were. We should've just killed him ourselves long before that." She shoved one of the brittle crackers into her mouth and gulped down a big sip from a bottle of water.

"I know but our patience paid off, now we know exactly what'll happen to us if we keep eating those fucking lemons. I'd rather die than go through what, Jake went through."

"You and me both."

"So, we need to head back to the plane today."

"Back to the plane?"

"We need to get Phoebe and Martin's bodies and bring them here."

"Who's Martin?"

"Martin was the pilot, dear…"

"Oh, right, Martin…" she pretended to recall his name but obviously didn't. Maybe it was to make herself somehow feel better?

"I still don't understand though, why do we need their bodies?"

"Because we're going to eat them. With three dead bodies, we should be able to last months. Well, Martin looked like he was mostly bones, but nonetheless, whatever we can scrape off him. Plus, Jake and Phoebe—I think that might be enough to get us through this. A plane has to come this way eventually…"

"Byron, honey, I love you but I'm not eating a fucking dead body. We have a good amount of food still and the lemons mixed in moderation should be able to last us another couple of weeks."

"Well, that's your choice I suppose, but what if they don't come by then? What then? You'll eventually die, right? And you will die much quicker than me if I'm eating these corpses. And once you're dead and the corpses run out, what then? If it comes down to it, should I eat you too? I mean if you died, of course, you wouldn't mind, would you?"

Sasha looked at him with a newfound repulsion. The man (and that seemed like a generous use of the word now) had no boundaries. He'd already been thinking about sinking his teeth into her, that alone was grimly concerning. She looked up at the clear blue sky and said a short prayer in her head for the planes to arrive soon. Otherwise, she knew a bad moon was on the rise.

***

The food ran out quicker than expected like they might have been eating a little more than they needed each day. Survival felt like some kind of bizarre rivalry at the point they'd reached. She could feel her body getting weaker, she could see herself beginning to progress into the tired heap that Jake had become.

There still hadn't seen a single plane in all the weeks they'd been there. She was growing a little concerned about Byron's food supply too. She slurped on the saliva-logged end of a lemon while his teeth gnawed into Jake's leathery hide. His ravenous eyes aimed at her while he feasted. He looked like a zombie but the fact she knew he was empowered with free will made the scenario even sicker to her.

Do you have to fucking look at me while you do that? Of course, you don't, so why are you? Is it some kind of message? Are you telling me what comes next? You disgust me.

His nonchalant, hideously-immoral behavior was something that she had to deal with every day now. His cannibalistic tendencies were more than a threat. That unsettled suspicion was only amplified by the fact that when they'd returned to wrangle the meat that both Phoebe and Martin had to offer at the crash site, the plane had inexplicably vanished.

Maybe a combination of the waves and undertow had somehow pulled it out. Anything was possible but it was odd that seemingly incredible events continued happening without warning. She could bend her principles of sanity to creatively justify and explain the plane disappearing, but how did the lemon trees keep blooming again overnight? Neither questioned it aloud, they'd stopped talking altogether. They just ate what they chose to and conserved their vigor.

As Sasha watched her husband's yellow teeth rip into Jake's gamey calf, she wondered: *That meat's running low, he's eating much more each day than he should. I've watched him chew tirelessly for four or five hours some days. The pickings are getting more minuscule by the minute. It looks rotten, it must be after being out in the sun all this time, I can smell that much. But like Jake said, there are no bugs… Why are there no bugs?*

The question somehow became relevant to her finally, maybe because there were no other questions to ask that could be answered in an optimistic manner. There was no hope at this stage. The things she was forced to watch every day were too ugly for her to believe that the conclusion could be anything but absolute horror. She looked away from the heartless barbarian she once loved and back up to the heavens.

God, please kill me before he does.

***

Sasha never did wake up. The first strike from Jake's picked-clean thighbone went right through her picture-perfect forehead and jammed into her brain.

She had been wondering where Byron had been disappearing off to over the last few days. He came back covered in sweat like he'd been working in a field all day. Now the answer she'd hungered for was stuck right into the section of her body that generated the query, in the form of a sharpened leg shard.

He had filed it to pinpoint accuracy by rubbing it

furiously against a rugged rock. The task was tedious but proved effective. She was already deceased when he removed the skeletal staff from her caved-in skull, but that wasn't the end. He beat her face in with the joint end until she was unrecognizable. Maybe that was his goal? Maybe he could avoid the guilt of eating the woman that he loved and promised to protect and care for in sickness and health. It was clear those heartfelt vows didn't apply in the no man's land they'd found themselves trapped within.

He cut her breast open with the polished side of his staff and removed her implants. He didn't want to bite down on something artificial or potentially toxic during one of his meals. He slumped under a lemon tree and played with the Jell-O bag like a child with his only toy.

Byron was happy with himself in his own sick way. *I did what I had to; she was dead soon anyway. I saved her from a long and excruciating demise. I did her a favor. I set her free. She won't have to experience what Jake did now. Thanks to me. Thanks to my good deed. I think it's time to celebrate.*

Byron set the bloody implant down beside him. He reached into his pocket and retrieved the same silver satanic tin that he'd stored the limbo capsules in on the airplane. He opened the box and tossed two inside his mouth and quickly swallowed them down dry.

"Can't believe they all actually stuck them inside their asses. Fucking idiots," he laughed to himself.

Even when swallowed, they hit almost immediately; the gel lining was designed to dissolve upon contact of nearly any type of fluid. The absurd truth had finally been exposed but everyone in his presence was too dead to comprehend it: Byron had been tripping the entire time. When his hallucinations began to taper off and he was feeling a little too normal, bam, he popped another. It made things easier.

As the meltdown returned with an even more jarring impact due to the double dose, the sky morphed into an exaggerated plum tone. The trees now seemed gargantuan and streamed high into the clouds. And in those lavender clouds and streaking trees was a familiar massive black craft.

It got bigger as it closed in on the island. *They're here to save me,* he thought staring at the pair of strange men at the edge of the platform. As the thought generated in his head, the beings vanished from their stage only to reappear directly before him in a blink.

Their shadowy forms were like dark cloths flapping in the wind, but as they spoke to Byron, they solidified. *You've done it, you are the winner, you are the champion, Byron. Congratulations.*

The telepathic transmission was music to his ears. A wide grin comprised his expression as the three of them levitated back up to the platform of the craft. In the span of a single second, the craft shot off up into the blurry atmosphere.

Instantly after the strange craft had vanished, the island began to rumble like an earthquake of seismic proportions was occurring. As the sand sifted away and the trees fell over, the island elevated from the waters and turned, creating an incline on the surface. All the dirt and plants slid off into the ocean water and sank to a salty end, revealing underneath another mammoth craft identical to the one that had just taken Byron.

Once it was off the ocean, it sped away following the path of its sister spaceship. The area it had previously occupied looked as if there had never been an island there at all. In the ship, two more shadowy figures used their minds to alter the screens and what they projected in front of them.

The various displays showed an array of visuals from the different perspectives of each of the people that had been on Byron's plane. From their trip to the crash to the island; every second was accounted for. They cut the footage with tremendous speed. It maybe took them two or three minutes to bundle and package the entire twenty-episode season of the increasingly popular otherworldly entertainment.

***

Long after the show had been released to the critical acclaim of the mysterious populous, Byron was still a celebrity. In a shadowy building, on their shadowy planet, inside a shadowy cage, is where Byron laid. His new home was a museum of sorts.

Whenever the unusual race wanted to visit him, they had the option of feeding a meager pinch of their currency to, in turn, feed Byron a lemon. It was a no-brainer. Nearly everyone who entered chose to relive the nostalgic thrill of his enjoyable win that had captured the strange web-like moist substance in their chests (their hearts).

The gimmick was so popular that it had forced Byron to eat so many lemons that he'd gone blind. Additionally, the acid-base he was forced to consume as part of his act had over time, rotted all of his teeth from his mouth. His gummy hole riddled grimace made him appear amused but he certainly wasn't. His stomach was peppered with white splotches as it had nearly turned into one giant bleeding ulcer.

His body shook uncontrollably from his vitamin deficiencies and he was unable to sleep due to the insomnia that he'd developed. His non-stop diarrhea and everlasting indigestion were scorching hardships; extra doses of endless pain that his new profession saw him endure all day and all night.

The horror and anguish of what he experienced made him recall when he was back on the island. When he told Sasha that he'd rather die than endure all that Jake had. He had gotten the best of both worlds. He died almost every day, but fortunately for the paying customer that wanted to see Byron, the unusual race's technology was advanced enough to patch up a decrepit rotting organism like Byron any time they desired to. It was sort of like jumping an old car battery. Each morning, before work, a shadowy maintenance figure started up Byron's deformed, haggard body and readied him to give the beings what they wanted.

Byron would have given anything for another few doses of limbo again; anything to get away from his gruesome suffering and enslavement. Although, since all he had left was time to think, he got around to wondering if maybe he still was in limbo. Somehow stuck in wherever it had brought him. Every day before he died each night, he couldn't help but reconfirm the fact that life had given him lemons… And it had left a permanent sour taste in his mouth.

THE SACRED COW

Zeke's mouth was dry as hell. He couldn't remember how long he'd been walking for exactly but the blazing sun and suffocating humidity had rapidly become worrisome. He staggered down the uninhabited dusty road, dangerously depleted. As a blinding sand cloud kicked up behind him, his mind allowed only the blurry dreams of ingesting water and nourishment to fester in his skull.

He wiped the coarse irritating dirt from his sights and did a doubletake when his eyes finally came upon the hand-carved wooden sign. It was hard to trust them in his state of extreme exhaustion. Ford Farm, as the sign had branded it, looked enormous. It held a wide variety of crops littered amongst the goliath acreage.

Additionally, there stood a sizable bundle of tall and oblong homestead structures. There had to be over a dozen of the well-maintained, modern buildings including barns, cow-sheds, chicken coops, stables, pigpens, silos, and a vast milking shack.

Zeke's excitement was uncontrollable. The sleepy drifter headed straight for the farmhouse with a new lively motivation now infused into his stride. He slid his bone-dry tongue over his cracked and peeling lips while laughing inside. *It's a miracle, a God damn miracle.*

A place as grandiose as Ford Farm undoubtedly had innumerable duties, ranches like it were usually always on the lookout for an extra hand or two. It was just the kind of place that could help him get back on his feet again. It was just the kind of place that he'd been daydreaming about.

When stepping onto the sturdy floorboards of the wrap-around country porch, his chest pounded with uncomfortable angst. He couldn't fuck up his lone opportunity; he needed to crush a home run out of the park and let management know he was a winner. He could get any job done without issue.

The weary wanderer's cracked and muddy knuckles hammered on the door like a last-ditch SOS. Almost immediately, the wooden barrier creaked open and an elderly, yet proud-looking man faced him. His wrinkled expression held no feeling as he tipped his cattleman hat at the stranger. "Mornin', sir, what brings you out my way?"

"Name's Zeke, Zeke Cutler," he replied sheepishly.

"Clayton Ford."

"Well, quite frankly, Mr. Ford, I'm lookin' for work. I happened to notice you've got quite the operation going on here. Seems a place like this can't have too much help I figure. I have years of experience tending to animals and looking after crops, and I can run most any kind of machinery."

Clayton looked him over again after spitting out his one-line resumé. The filth upon him was repulsive, his stench was potent. He was certainly not the first man you'd want to rub elbows with. His silence continued a bit longer, becoming uncomfortable.

It was probably the pity that fueled him to open the door further. "Why don't you take a seat at the table there," he pointed.

Zeke did as he was told then watched Clayton limp over to the refrigerator. *The old man looks wounded, he could definitely use the help*, Zeke thought. He studied him carefully as he reached into the cooling container and removed a full jug of milk. He pulled a clear glass from the dishrack and set it down beside him. He returned with a plate of leftover veggies and ham from the prior evening, and slid the heaping portion over to the disheveled nomad with a friendly smile.

He was beyond ecstatic to wet his whistle and get a belly-full of sustenance but suddenly that wasn't Zeke's primary focus anymore. Just before the old man shut the door of the fridge, his dry eyes caught a glimpse of something odd. Inside the chilling unit, on the left side, was a steel lockbox that was mysteriously bonded to the appliance's interior. The reflective chrome shined like something special and the keyhole gaped; like it was calling to him.

"You go ahead and eat and drink up. Have as much as you like, but unfortunately, the farm has all the help it needs for the time being."

Zeke was shocked by the response. "Mr. Ford, if you don't mind me askin', how many workers do you have helping you here?"

Clayton squared his eyes and zeroed in on him carefully. "Just me. I'm all this place needs."

***

Zeke knew for certain the old son of a bitch was lying through his false teeth. One man alone wasn't capable of tending to so many animals and completing the myriad of tasks required to keep a place like that cranking. His own involvement and personal experience with the duties of a farmhand told him that much. Especially a fragile-looking, withered bone-bag like Farmer Ford. To suggest something so illogical to a seasoned man of his experience was absurd and frankly, it bordered on disrespectful. Something was going on. The farmer was hiding something, and he needed to find out what.

After an evening of calm rejuvenation that included drinking from the water hose outside and poaching some extra eats from Farmer Ford's crops, Zeke was finally starting to feel right again. His cognitive senses were back to normal and the aches that ailed him were no longer pulsating through most of his body.

He sat perched in the brush watching the entire farm like a hawk; the old bastard had been upstairs in the farmhouse for some time now. He would wait to see him operate no matter how long it took. He would eventually reveal the truth, it was just a matter of time.

After all of the light-bulbs on the second floor cut out, the moon glowed eerily and became the lone light source. Suddenly, he heard some creaking noises that sounded like footsteps on an old wooden staircase. He peered through the window to see Clayton standing over by the fridge again. He carefully opened the cat-shaped cookie jar sitting on the counter to his right and removed a key that was taped under the ceramic top.

Zeke waited keenly with anticipation as he unlocked the steel box to reveal four capped but empty glass bottles. The farmer removed the glass set and placed them into a small milk crate before closing the fridge back up and making his way to the door.

Zeke scurried into the tall crops and made himself vanish out of sight but not without vantage point. He continued to study his target and listened carefully to each of his hobbling footsteps. When it sounded like they were a safer distance from his hiding spot, he cautiously peeped through the thick stalks of vegetation.

Clayton used the same key as before to unlock the brick-stained bulkhead. As the metal door slammed into the dirt, the farmer stepped inside. He descended the steps, sealing the opening behind him.

He was probably down there for close to an hour

all the while Zeke couldn't help but wonder what exactly he would be doing in his thoughtfully-locked basement at that time of night. Playing the role of the ever-patient stalker, his mind expanded, secreting more queries to echo inside his head. *What the hell is going on here? What's this weird fucker up to now? Why would he leave empty glass bottles locked with such attention inside of a fridge?*

His torrent of thoughts was finally interrupted by the farmer's reemergence from the underground. Zeke eyed him carefully as he locked up again and eventually made his way back to the kitchen.

His liver-spotted hands set the milk crate down on the table and yanked on the refrigerator handle. He retrieved the now-brimming bottles from the crate and was offered an improved glimpse at their contents. The interior dome light beamed down on the substance in the freshly occupied containers. The foreign liquid bubbled sluggishly and was as murky as hot tar. He set three of the vile refreshments back into the lockbox and turned the key, ensuring their security.

The tired rancher unscrewed the one he'd set aside and poured the sickening gloom down his throat. It took some active swallowing and waiting for the final drops of the molasses-like mess to crawl out, but eventually, it was empty. He rinsed out the container in methodical fashion and promptly returned the key to its previous hiding spot.

Without warning, Clayton was moving faster than Zeke's vision could track. He wasn't taking steps; he was somehow just appearing in places. In a matter of seconds, he'd washed, dried, and put away a sink full of dishes, cleaned the stove, table, and counter in addition to sweeping the floor. Every chore in the room was complete in less than a minute.

Zeke didn't see him actually do it all. It was so quick, it happened in flashes like some kind of lightspeed time-lapse. The impossible movements manifesting before him were shattering his concept of physics. The entire world as he had known it was suddenly a far different place.

Zeke knew he needed to get out of dodge. At the lawbreaking pace the farmer was stirring about at, there was no telling when the pruned bastard might sneak up behind him. If he were to be discovered spying on him during this supernatural sequence, there was no telling how he might react or what he was capable of.

He made a decision in haste and dove behind some bushes close to the house and perked his ears up listening intently. A rustling noise started emanating from the crops. The unexplainable actions had picked up in the cornfield where they had left off in the kitchen.

An empty flatbed appeared twenty or so yards away from him and was filled with harvested produces, shucked and all, in less than fifteen minutes. From the cornfield, he moved into the milking shed, draining them all in record time. He flashed between each of the cattle with such speed and grace before moving on to collect eggs from the chickens.

He went on like that for hours, completing what would have been a full days' work for nearly a dozen men. The phenomenon was a power like no other Zeke had ever witnessed. The tier of power that came with his abilities was mind-jarring. Forget about running a fucking farm, if Zeke could get his hands on that kind of power, he'd be running the fuckin world.

Son of a bitch was right; he is all this place needs. But what about my needs? He tried to buy me off with a shitty plate of hog and a couple of glasses of milk. Can't throw this dog off the trail though, nope. This dog hunts. I'm gonna find it, your secret's gonna be mine, old man. You being greedy, you can't have something that special all to yourself, no, sir...

Whatever that black shit is will certainly be worth a pretty fuckin' penny. Forget about money, I could play fuckin' God himself if I had that. Hell, I could fuck every girl and they wouldn't even know it. I could live the experiences of a thousand men if I only had it.

***

Zeke stood over the bulkhead and unbolted the sliding lock. After watching the old farmer's blinding speed tend to the farm all night, he'd finally retired. The key wasn't difficult to get. The trusting elder left his doors open, after all, he was in the middle of nowhere. He knew a minimal stash of the magical fluid lay in the icebox but the true prize was subterranean.

Once inside, he entered a tunnel that only led in one direction. Upon reaching the end, he was met with a cracked steel door with a red radiance filling the gap. Grunts of discomfort and struggle could be heard clearly. Even with spiking agony as the soundtrack seeping toward him, still, he needed to know.

The payoff was so great that he'd gladly sacrifice his own pathetic existence to have a chance at to wield the wonders he'd seen. He pushed the door open softly, only to be confronted with another impossible view. The hellish room was lined with a dozen or so stables on each side. But the horror housed dead center of the secretive operation left him statuesque.

While the creature held cow-like fur patterns and bovine features, in Zeke's gut, he knew it couldn't be. A mouth the size of his torso lined the thing's ribcage. Its lone eye was the size of a basketball with the cloudy cornea melded into its marbled huffing nose. Its udder was fat and filled to distortion, on the verge of bursting while the phallus fashioned teats gyrated with unnatural alacrity.

Its cavernous pit began to throb, allowing a deep look into the thing's oblivion. Drool sloped from the trio of tongues patched together like grandma's handmade quilt. They flailed energetically.

"Caught her at supper," Clayton's voice confided.

Zeke turned around to see the farmer grasping a jagged sickle, a dribble of the darkness smeared around his lips. Before he could respond, both his hands and feet found the floor. It transpired so swiftly that there was no blood. He was suddenly confined to a cage with four nubs where the skin at the end had been seared shut along with his lips.

"Always keep a spare," he said pocketing the key

Clayton dragged a girl out from one of the stables. She looked terrified as she tried to scream with no tongue while staring at the abomination beside her. Her belly was plump with life as Clayton used the tip of the sickle to brutally C-section her stomach. A sinister enjoyment bubbled within him.

"Maybe I might have some work here for you after all. You see, my seed ain't what it used to be. I been havin' a little trouble getting these girls where they need to be." Crimson rushed from the shaking woman's belly as Clayton found his sinister grin.

"You think you got what it takes to fill one of these ladies up every month? We gotta keep 'em coming steady you know. I got a lotta work that needs doing around here, can't afford any screw-ups." He paused a moment as if awaiting a response from him.

Zeke just breathed in and out from his nostrils manically like a crazed stallion running into war. Snot flurried out, splattering below over his orifice filled with recently melted flesh. His tears welled up, he'd come so close, so very close.

"Well, I guess time'll tell. We'll find out soon if you got what it takes there, son. I stagger 'em you see, I depend on them so I needn't depend on anyone else. I have to always make sure I have enough of them for precious here," he said, patting the fuzzy atrocity like it was his kin.

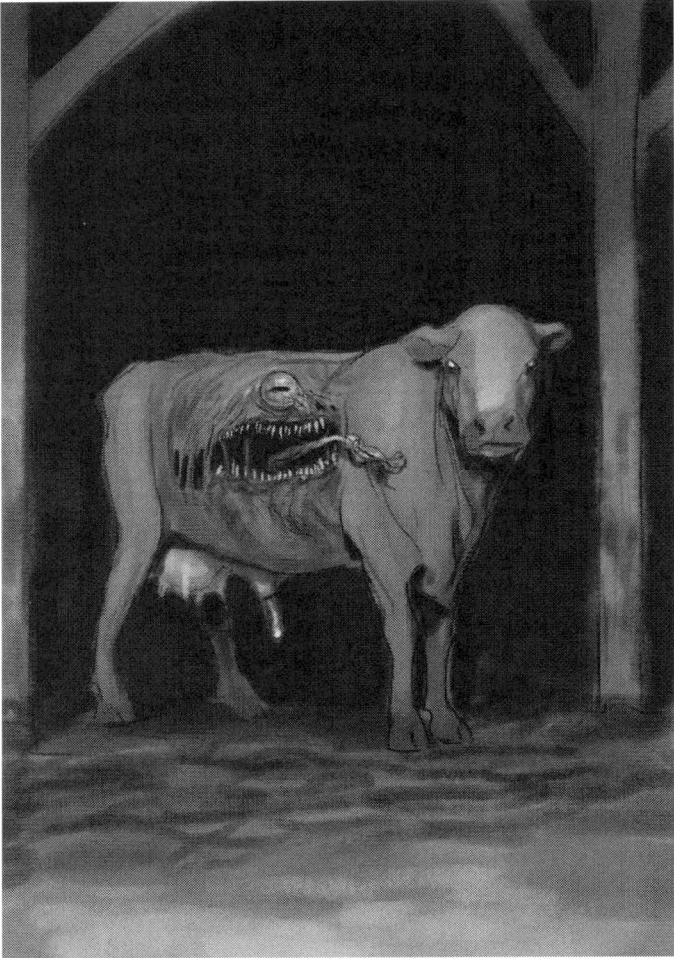

The shrieking baby fell out with the girl's gut but in an instant, her abdomen was sewn back together and good as new. Clayton regulated the tormented woman back to her designated stall no different than if she were livestock coming in from the pasture.

He picked the gory baby off the cold, muddy floor by its foot and examined its health momentarily. It seemed to be just starting to understand how breathing worked when Clayton tossed it, kicking and squirming, into the eager slobbering monstrosity. The gargantuan teeth crushed the newborn to a youthful pulp, leeching the essence, while its teats secreted a waterfall of warm, black milk into the pail beneath.

RUMORS

When freshman year started, Chelsea made a promise to herself. By the time she became a senior, she would be the most revered and sought-after girl in the school. It wouldn't be a hard task; she had already matured physically and looked more like a woman than most of her upper classmates. She was content and stable, so long as every boy dreamed about being with her and stood obediently salivating over her beauty.

That was the case at the start of the year until Violet, the new girl, joined their class. An unbiased eye could easily tell that Chelsea was less than thrilled in seeing the extra attention that was normally aimed at her get redirected. Violet was just about as pretty as she was but her untamed hair was stunning. It shimmered in the light and held the kind of bounce and volume that Chelsea could only dream about.

Chelsea decided instead of watching the new girl try to replace her, she would use her influence to put an end to the competition. She sought out the chattiest girls that she knew of and told them how she'd seen a whole family of buff lice crawling throughout Violet's gorgeous mane. The girls were in shock and disgusted by the thought that they, too, could be exposed to the squirm-worthy skull parasites.

In a matter of days, much of the class could be heard snickering behind her back, the jokes and cruelty at her expense wouldn't stop with words. They drew pictures of her with the bugs crawling all over her and taped them to her locker. Slowly, but surely, the number of lovesick boys that were previously enamored by her presence had dwindled down to zero. Even the other girls that were friendly and enjoyed Violet's company had been forced to turn their backs on her. They didn't want to get bugs or be accused of such for hanging around her.

Chelsea loved what she was seeing; the attention of the cute boys had been readdressed back to her and she'd watched in relief as Violet tumbled down the social pecking order. It was difficult enough coming from another school and blending in. Standing out could be a good thing at times but Violet wasn't standing out in the way anyone would hope. She had been smeared by her peers, ruined in her own eyes, but that still wasn't good enough for Chelsea.

After school one day, she stopped at the pharmacy and bought a bottle of hair removal cream. She walked in the moonlight to Violet's house and waited patiently outside. Even after all the lights in the house went off, she waited a little longer. Finally, once she believed everyone was sound asleep, she crept into her house through the basement window. She carefully navigated her way to the bathroom and eyed the shower cell. She grabbed the shampoo bottle and dumped the contents in the trash, replacing it with the removal cream.

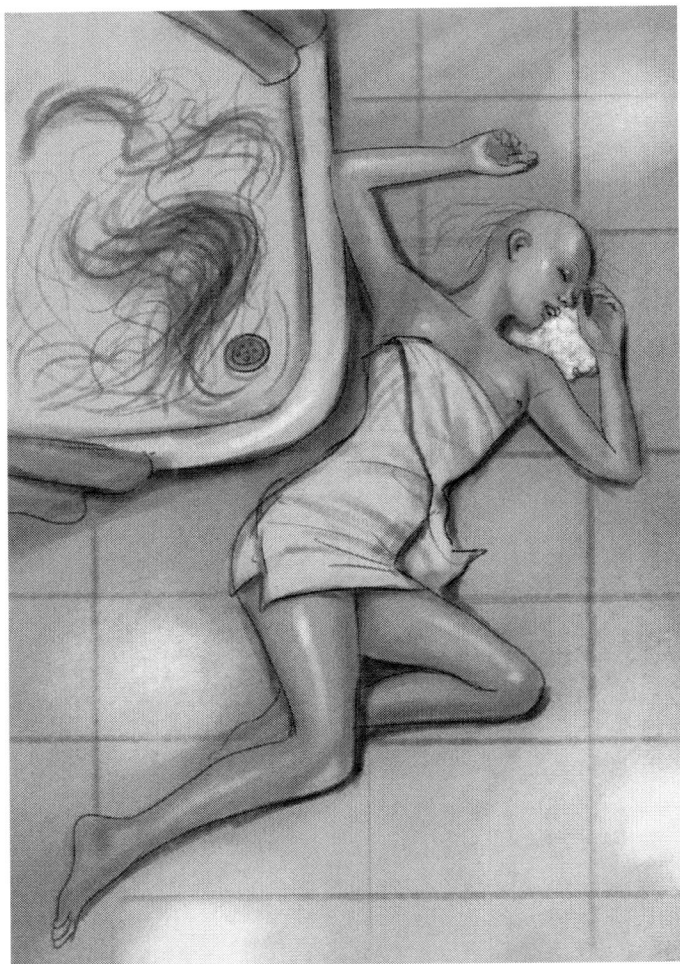

The next morning, Violet never showed up to class. The students eventually found out that nearly all of the poor girl's hair had fallen out in the shower. After seeing the vast clump of her once-gorgeous black mane in the shower drain, she'd taken every pill in the medicine cabinet and fallen asleep... Forever.

It wasn't enough that Chelsea knew the girl was ruined and had taken her own life, she wanted to see for herself. She attended Violet's funeral and laughed to herself at the sight of her stiff, pale corpse with a patchwork head. Her family hadn't enough money or mental stability to suggest a wig for their sad child's dead body. She fed off the hurt in her parents' eyes with a dark delight and fascination.

The rest of Chelsea's freshman year continued just as she'd hoped; she was the centerpiece of everything. She'd made good on her promise; she was a seductive fantasy to every boy and feared by every girl. While no one knew that she was directly responsible for Violet's demise, they knew her hands couldn't be entirely clean. They noticed the spite and venom that she'd tarnished Violet's reputation with, they knew she wasn't distraught by her indefinite departure.

Over the summer, she felt proud at all that she'd accomplished, and going into her sophomore year she felt unstoppable. Until another newcomer named Jessica filled the spot that Violet had previously. Jessica was even more stunning than Violet. Even though she wore glasses, that didn't stop anyone from admiring the hypnotic blue eyes she had.

They were the prettiest blue eyes that Chelsea had ever seen, and it didn't take long for the boys to switch their seats and get lost in them. She loathed watching them follow her around aimlessly like little puppy dogs.

She hated watching them stare into her eyes as she sucked them in deeper like some kind of gorgeous black hole.

Chelsea began to spread her whispers again; she harassed her with childish taunts like *nerd* and *four-eyes*. Others eventually followed her lead and joined in. It continued day after day like incessant torture until one morning, Jessica arrived minus her glasses. Chelsea balled up a sheet of loose-leaf and looked up at her grinning. "Now four-eyes can't see!" she yelled, tossing the paper ball at her face.

To Chelsea's astonishment, Jessica caught the paper with legendary reflex and sent it flying right back at her. It smacked her on the head and everyone began to laugh hysterically. Chelsea sat quietly for once, her face turning a sinking shade of red as she bottled her rage.

She had already plotted her revenge by the time they got out of school. Chelsea returned home and went into the washroom with a small plastic bottle. She filled it up a bit with bleach and then set off for Jessica's house. She waited outside silently, just as she did at Violet's house, for all the lights to go out and the occupants to slip into slumber.

Once she believed that was the case, Chelsea snuck inside. She quietly made her way to the bathroom and located Jessica's contact case. They were inside sitting in the sanitizing solution before Chelsea partially drained each side. She dropped in just a bit of the bleach into each plastic crater, making sure the contacts were coated before capping them off.

The next morning, no one saw Jessica but even sadder was that Jessica never saw them either, or anyone else ever again... The stinging toxic chemical destroyed both of her pupils and left her completely blind in both eyes. Everyone at school heard that she would be returning soon but was in the process of being shifted to a special needs class that could better accommodate her disability. Little did they know the young girl would never be able to waltz down the checkered hallways of their school again.

Due to her blindness, it was difficult for the medical examiner to determine if Jessica simply fell down the stairs or threw herself, but regardless of what had set her in motion, she had snapped her neck and died instantly. Her parents heard the tumble and arrived to find her laying in her own blood with her head cracked open and gaping.

At the funeral, Chelsea was again quite amused at her handiwork. She might not have turned her eyeballs white and busted open Jessica's brain herself but she felt a fair share of responsibility. She stared at the lifeless teen and felt reassured that the next two years should be a cakewalk. Jessica was quite defiant and she doubted that anyone so bold would cross her again.

When junior year rolled around, Chelsea went through her usual formality and examined the school roster for any potential threats. She wasn't surprised to see that there was another student that would be joining their class again this year. Amanda was every bit as cute as Chelsea, but her smile was absolutely flawless. Just a few perks of the dimples and her pearly grin was free. Her sparkling teeth made every boy in class want to stick their tongue in her mouth, and rather quickly they were doing just that.

Chelsea's smile wasn't awful; Amanda's was just mesmerizing. She dreaded every day thinking about how her happiness brought a spark to those around her. How a simple curl of her lips would see them flock to her. How they all tried to make her laugh since they enjoyed it so much.

It irritated her to such an extreme, that for a third time now, Chelsea sought out her pawns. She told them that her teeth weren't real, that she was born with a strange birth defect that left her with just gums. She had to get dentures and her mouth smelled like old people. She did her best to damage her status but the outlandish rumors did little damage.

Chelsea decided it was time to take action. She began to follow Amanda and watch what fridge she put her lunch into. Once she knew her habit, she snuck down into the cafeteria one day before lunch. She removed her lunch bag and found a sandwich inside. She quickly peeled back the bread and stuck a handful of screws and bolts into the tuna fish mix.

Later during lunch period, she took a seat in close proximity to Amanda, making certain she had a good vantage point to watch. She watched her striking smirk flash as she unwrapped her tuna sandwich. She was close enough to see one of her incisors crack in half as it went full bore into an unforgiving screw. Amanda shrieked out in pain as the blood and ruptured enamel fell from her mouth all over the mushy sandwich.

She was out of school for a few days but the dentist had patched her up; one of her teeth had been extracted and replaced while two others had been capped. She wondered who the dentist was as they did an excellent job. It was hard to tell she'd suffered any trauma. She'd have to find out but before she could focus on that, she needed to finish the task at hand.

There was no subtle way through this one… There was no chemical that she could use or easy way to get a tooth out. This year would be different; she would have to face the problem head-on. She found a hammer near the workbench in her basement and tucked it deep in her backpack.

The following morning, she surveyed Amanda without fail. She knew that she couldn't do anything to her at school, but once the bell rang, Chelsea tailed her.

She maintained a far enough distance that she never looked back. As Amanda entered the woods to take a shortcut home, she saw her golden opportunity. She removed the hammer from her bag and ran up to her.

By the time Amanda turned around, it was too late. The claw end crashed into her mouth, destroying everything the dentist had fixed and so much more. The strike stunned her as she coughed out fragments of her chompers and crimson all over the grass. The next blow from the pointed side put her out cold, and the third and final one readied her for the morgue.

Chelsea was a little sad at the funeral. The condition she'd left Amanda's face in wasn't anything appropriate for friends and family to view. The casket was closed, leaving her unable to get a gander at her impression. She pushed aside the thought and tried to instead focus on the future. Next year would be her final year in school, then it was off to hurting people in the workplace more than likely. She was growing up. The idea made her wistful overall, but there was still a murmur of enthusiasm for what came next.

Senior year was far different than the rest; people seemed to separate, form their own cliques, and drift away from the previously tight nucleus that they'd built over time. Additionally, the new girl, Tina, that joined the class wasn't even pretty. She was ugly as a pig's rear and not a single one of her features posed any threat to Chelsea. She didn't pursue any of the boys, she, instead, just focused on her work and spent much of her time after school in the science lab.

The geek wasn't even worth it to Chelsea—Tina wasn't in her league. Chelsea had become bored by the whole ritual, especially now that the challenge had died. For most of the year, she just focused on her studies and daydreamed about the fictitious people that she might meet and drive to their end post-graduation.

After a mostly uneventful year, one day after school, Tina caught up with her during her walk home. Chelsea was surprised by the interaction and wondered what she could possibly want. "I heard a rumor about you," Tina said.

"Yeah, a lot of those seem to float around at school, so what?"

"Is it true?"

"Is what true?"

"Are you the reason those other girls that joined the school are all dead?"

"Keep asking dumb questions and you might find out."

"They said you didn't bother killing me because I'm ugly. Am I not worthy of your effort?"

"It's true, yes, you are so worthless that I can't bring myself to even try and hurt you. Not even a sliver of you is better than my most damaged area. In fact, after meeting you, I'm not sure I can ever hurt anyone again.

I want to—I daydream about it—but I just don't know anymore…"

"What about my brain? I'm much smarter than you. Couldn't you destroy my brain?"

"I suppose I could," Chelsea replied, a bit confused at the bizarre nature of her request.

"Will you then?"

"Perhaps, I don't know, I'm not sure that I value your intelligence the same way I did Jessica's eyes or Amanda's smile. That was motivation, but tell me, why are you in such a rush to die anyway?"

"That's none of your business now, is it? I'm simply asking for my due, I just want to be treated equally to my peers. Is that too much to ask?"

"In a way, yes. What I did to those girls was out of my love for cruelty and, of course, my own selfishness. It seems the suffering I've generated in overlooking you is more painful than any beating I could offer. So, if I ended your life, it's like I'd be doing you a favor and myself a disservice. Does that register with your big brain? Are you smart enough to figure that one out?"

"Yes."

"So, if you want to die, you will need to do it yourself, understood?"

There was a brief silence before Tina pushed the issue. "What if I killed you instead?" she threatened.

"Is that a hypothetical or are you threatening me?"

"I wasn't sure at first but now I've decided," she extracted a gigantic blade from her bag. "I will cut your throat where we stand if you don't agree."

"Okay, fuck it, I'll kill you, just put that thing away."

Tina obeyed her wish as a smile crossed her face for the first time in what seemed like forever. "Okay then, in one week, we can meet in the woods. It'll be best if we do it there, I don't want you to get in trouble." Chelsea turned and continued home when Tina's voice suddenly started up again. "Oh, and Chelsea, thank you. I promise you won't regret killing me."

***

One week later, Chelsea headed into the woods like she said she was going to. Tina had slipped her a note in study hall that they should hike out a little further near a patch of swampland. She came upon Tina sitting Indian-style, her book bag on one side of her, and a frizzled potato sack covering something on the other. She slapped a mosquito that had started to suck on her neck and stood up.

"I'm glad you could make it," Tina extended her blood-smeared hand in greeting.

Chelsea overlooked the gesture and said, "Let's just get on with it already."

"Right," Tina replied turning to the swamp, "I picked this spot because once I'm dead, you can just dump me into these green waters. I figure the alligators, snappers, and snakes would eat me up pretty quickly, which leaves less evidence to tie you to this. I want you to decapitate me with my knife here," she instructed, removing it from her bag before handing it over to her.

"Just stick your knee in my back while you're sawing through my throat. That should ensure most of the blood falls in with my body," Tina surmised.

"What about your head?" Chelsea inquired.

"Well, remember how I was saying my brain is probably my most valuable asset? You can probably use the knife handle to crack my skull and pull it apart.

Once you get it open, I want you to take my brain out. After you've done that, just throw the pieces of my head in with the body. You can probably toss the knife in there too. I brought a couple of bottles of water for you to wash your hands off with afterward."

"Thanks. Okay, you about ready then? I have dinner in literally an hour."

"Yeah, I'm ready. Oh wait, one more thing. I got something for you on the count of you agreeing to kill me. I know I kind of had to threaten you a little and I apologize for that, which is why I pushed this killing out one week so I could prepare."

"Prepare for what?"

"I made you a gift," Tina said, bending down and reaching under the potato sack. She pulled out a severed head that looked to be in rough shape. Its pieces were stitched ruggedly like a mad scientist had gotten hold of it. "I took the parts of those girls that you hated the most and put them together for you. I got a little bit of everything here."

Chelsea looked at the spoiled tissue in amazement. The girls were relatively fresh, the maggots and worms hadn't gotten to the decaying flesh yet. She held onto the dangling necrotic offering by only a handful of hairs that remained from Violet's wrinkly, balding scalp which had been sewn onto the top half of Jessica's head. It was easy to tell it was hers since the back of the skull was busted open from her fall down the stairs, and the eyeballs were that of a dead blind girl; pale and sunk into their sockets. The lower section of Amanda's region was stapled onto Jessica's portion. The wrecked and mutilated mouth was a sight for sore eyes. Chelsea nearly became emotional at the sight; one she'd been deprived of at the girl's closed casket funeral.

"This is… This is the nicest thing anyone's ever done for me, thank you so much," Chelsea held back the tears but was showing her hand.

"The last part is your choice. I left the gaping hole in the back of Jessica's head open because, if you think I'm deserving, I'd like you to put my brain inside."

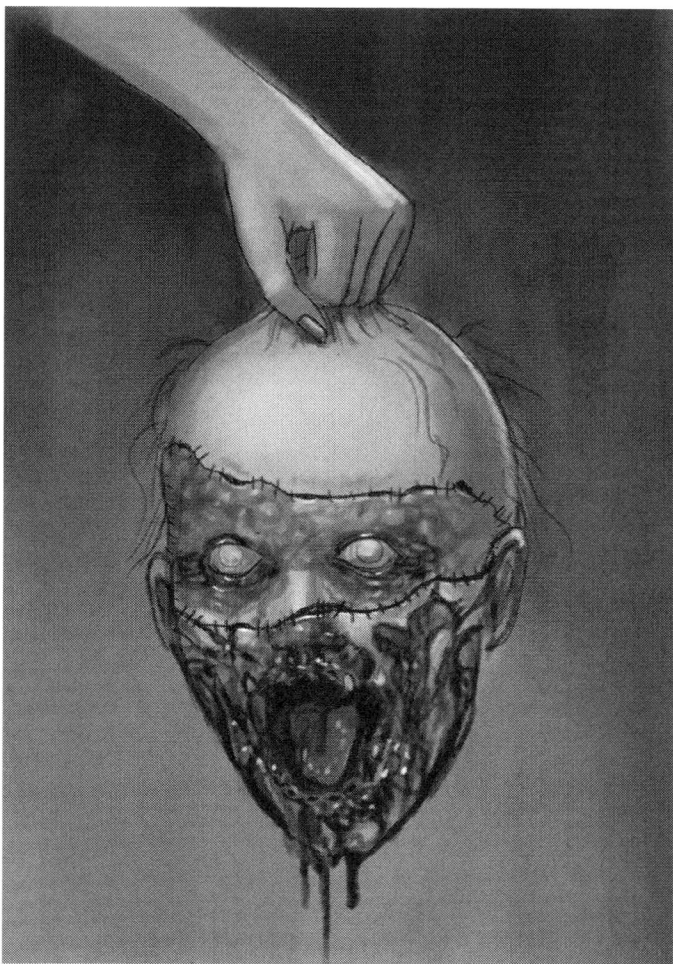

"I'll think about it," Chelsea said sternly.

"Fair enough."

"One last question, why is it still bloody? They've been dead for some time."

Slipping up her sleeve Tina revealed a bandaged area on her forearm. "I used some of my own blood."

An unexpected twinkle of sorrow glimmered in Chelsea's eye as Tina got on her knees in front of the motionless alligators. Chelsea was feeling different suddenly. It was almost like she was going to miss her. As she grabbed hold of her hair and began to saw repeatedly against Tina's pale neck, the exposure of her slimy meat caused a tear to well up in her eye. She kicked Tina's still twitching frame into the murky waters and while the gators went to town, she began to beat on her head with the knife handle.

Her lips were still quivering when she dug out the brain like a peanut from its shell. She kicked what remained of her head into the murky waters with the rest of her body and then turned her attention the mummified intersect of violence she unleashed over the past four years. The swamp life quickly pounced on the gore-covered floating head, cherishing the unlikely opportunity, but Chelsea paid no attention.

The gift was so beautiful that she decided she would honor Tina's last wish. She slipped her brain inside the empty head, turning some of it to mush as she forced it through the messy, jagged opening. She tossed the keepsake into the gnarly potato sack, then left the marsh behind for good.

She found an excellent hiding spot in the woods for the head since the police would no doubt be searching for Tina soon. She stuck it up inside the chimney of an abandoned house not far from where she lived.

Every so often when she was feeling down, she'd go back to the old house, usually with materials for a picnic. She would spread a beach blanket out on the roach-infested floor and take the head out and have lunch with it. First, she would usually try to guess how many rodents or vermin would scurry out from it when she set it down. Then they'd reminisce about how stupid they were in high school. "Remember when I put those screws in your tuna fish?!" she laughed, eating a bite of the sandwich clenched in her murderous hands. She imagined the head would be laughing, too, if it was able to.

Chelsea never killed or drove anyone else to suicide after Tina; their dealings with each other appeared to evolve her. School was almost over and there was not much left to do except chat. In a way, she wished Tina was around. For the first time, she felt like talking with her.

She took a seat beside a few girls that she always gossiped with, knowing it could be the last time they would.

"Did you see Jenny? Oh my God, she's so gross! She smells like a dumpster fire on a hot day. Speaking of a dumpster fire, did they ever find that nerdy girl? What was it, Lina?" one of the girls remarked.

"Her name was Tina. I don't think she's coming back. I get the feeling she's some kinda runaway," Chelsea interjected.

"Probably thinks she can make it on her own cuz she's sooooooo smart. What a stupid bitch!" All the girls laughed except Chelsea.

After the chuckles died off, Chelsea locked onto them. "Do you want to know something that's absolutely fucking crazy about her?"

They nodded and leaned in closer acting as if they were prepared to protect the reveal. As they inched toward the edge of their seats they couldn't help but squirm with anticipation.

"Seriously though, you can't tell anyone, okay?"

"Yessssss! Just tell us already!"

"She was actually pretty cool."

OUTSIDE THE BOX

As I laid on the table, my body's static state forced me to listen to their banter. "Frank, you know he can still see and hear us, don't you?" Patricia explained, squeezing out the last few CCs of mystery fluid into my limp arm.

"I thought you said it would shut him down entirely?"

"Well yes, breathing, heartbeat, even body temp and texture should all emulate a postmortem state, but during the experiments, my consciousness never faded."

"I guess that adds another point to the undying metaphysical argument, but please tell me you only played the guinea pig in a virtual environment, right?

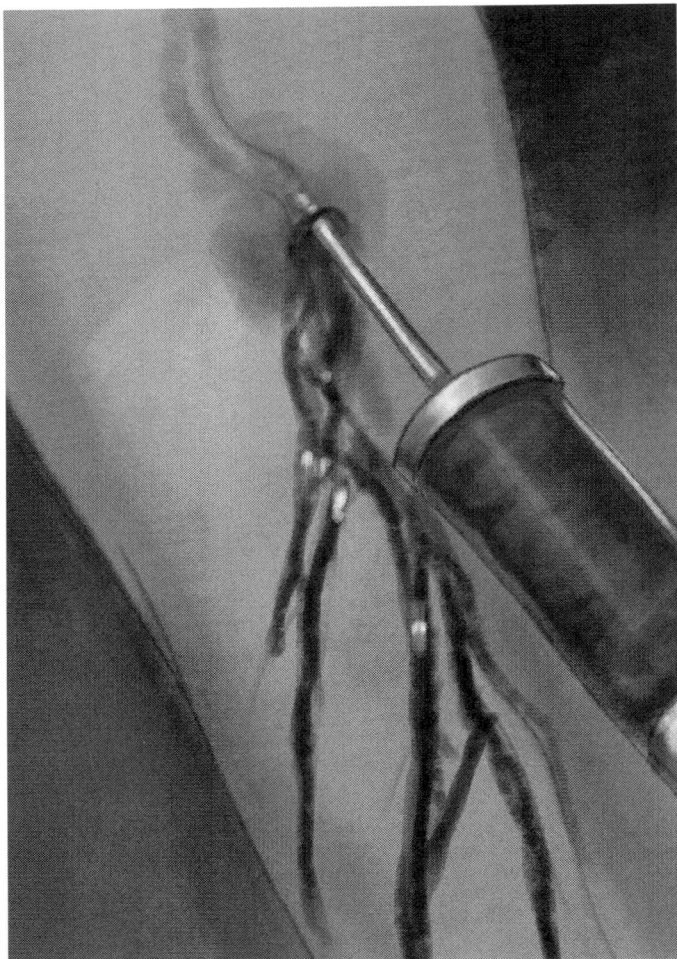

There was silence between them. "Patty, tell me you didn't actually inject yourself with that shit. We could've found another way."

Ugh, he called her Patty. The handful of times I'd lobbed that nickname her way, she wasn't shy about letting me know she hated it. She must really be into him. Either that or she's just not comfortable enough to scold him yet. Does he really think trusting a woman that would do this to her own husband is a good idea? What the hell is wrong with him?

"Of course, the testing was virtual, I could never risk being without you, my love, no matter how minor the threat is." It was hard to tell if she was lying. Patricia had already deceived me; the person closest to her for the last decade and done so in flawless fashion. Still, my gut told me she was far too selfish to test it on herself, but she was correct about the outcome—she knew I was aware.

Her fingers dropped the syringe into the metallic tray and she pressed her mouth against Frank's. They clawed at each other savagely like two teens that had been told they couldn't date each other. Their passion was nauseating; I would've blown chunks all over both of them if my body had permitted. A saliva trail dissipated as their lips pulled apart and Frank began to theorize.

"Well, maybe the software's algorithm was created by some whack-job religious zealot. There seems to be a lot of those characters in the computer field. These programs aren't as rigid and defined as a calculator, they can only predict what we already know or what we would potentially believe. This doesn't have you thinking there's something after now, does it?"

"Who knows, just because he can see and hear doesn't unequivocally mean his soul's serving as the receptor. An equally far-fetched assumption could simply be that my formula doesn't affect the brain. For the record, I hope he can see, hear, and feel every damn bit of this. If there was a way for me to peel his scalp back and check, I would've already."

Patricia locked in the lifelog equipment over my sternum. I felt the frigid cold of the metal and some pinching. The light on the device started out green before falling into a deep red. The readout on the flat-screen displayed the words in a digital font: Subject Deceased - Disposal Approved. They had successfully manipulated my biology enough to trick the device into approving of my discarding. The ship's arms positioned a single titanium casket and activated the purge pod. They wanted to send me off quickly, so no soul would ever learn the injustices surrounding my now seemingly inevitable demise.

When Patricia had slipped her little experimental concoction into my powdered nutrients, initially, I'd become quite calm. While my flesh's docile status was unpreventable, my mind was left to carelessly roam free. Surely, when people are aware that they're about to die they panic? Terror, dread, fear, regret, and gloom were all emotions that should have been thrashing about inside me, trying to push their way out like a caterpillar from its warm, comforting cocoon. If my sober calm was drug-induced, it would certainly be a pity when I came down and my equilibrium returned. The notion was a realization, not a fear, even though that seemed more rational.

As they loaded my stiff form into the unforgiving space coffin, the atmosphere was casual as a cup of coffee. "But back to my point, since it's probable that our friend, Irwin, here can still hear us, would you mind giving me a moment?" she asked, patting my pulseless chest. Frank seemed a bit confused by the request. "I'll finish up here, I just have a few parting words that's all," she looked like she required clearance which he reluctantly extended to her in the form of a nod.

Frank exited through the sliding metal door as Patricia looked me in the eyes while I remained paralyzed and at her mercy. This should be good; I could see her expression shift. Patricia didn't want her new partner to understand the acidic venom she could spit without warning. Not that she would ever do this to Frank but who knows, I'm sure when she met me, she didn't think this was how we'd say goodbye. Maybe since stumbling upon that revelation, it motivated her to prepare long in advance now.

She was probably just protecting her own wicked way of thinking; she couldn't show him all she was capable of. Just on the off chance that over time her precious Frank turned into Irwin 2.0.

"It's time you understand what I felt when I gifted you the best years of my life, you ungrateful primate. You might have been beside me, Irwin, but you were a ghost. You gave me absolutely nothing and I gave you everything." Tears watered down; her sobs were promoted by rage, not guilt or glumness. "It wasn't how you said things would be, you lied to me! So, it's time for you to know what it's like to be alone now. Your solitary ways will be permanent until the injections I gave you finally wear off. Until your body slowly unwinds back to what it was. Until you reanimate and slowly suffocate by yourself, floating and rotting through space for eternity."

What a crazy bitch. How sick and perverse does someone have to be to think of a scheme of this nature? Even for her, it seemed just a bit much.

As she pressed the button to commence my ejection from the ship, she left me with one final piece of information, "And there was enough in those needles to last for YEARS. I want you to have plenty of time

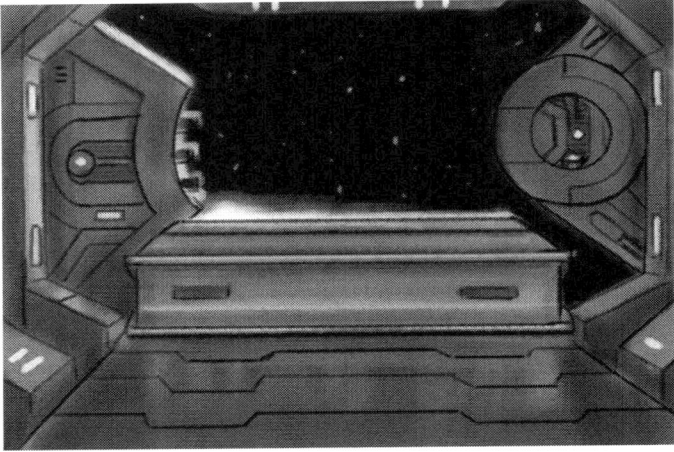

to yourself. Time to think, time to stress, and time to exhaust yourself and panic in your mind over and over again. You shall never cease the thought that, at any given moment, death may finally come for you. Or maybe I've surprised you and made it all up; maybe this period of suspended animation will be over by the end of the day. Maybe the reaper is much closer than you think. Either way, you'll find out soon... Or not."

The assistance arms of the craft automatically closed the lid, forcing me into the darkness and absolute isolation. I felt the container being moved onto the conveyer-belt within the purge pod, which would ultimately serve to expel me from the vessel. All of a sudden, I felt as though I'd been tipped off the edge of something. Gravity's grip relinquished entirely, and my body began to levitate within the expiration capsule.

Somehow, I still remained void of fear and most any emotion. Judging by the vindictive speech Patricia had given me upon sendoff, that must have been an unintentional side-effect. If there was one silver-lining to salvage from what should have been a horrifying situation, it was that at the very least, for the moment, I was as high as helium. I'm sure, like she said, when it all wears off, the initial burst of terror itself might kill me before I even run out of air. But until then, I'm riding the wave and all that noise about me sweating the moment death finds me doesn't seem as scary as I'm sure she intended it to be.

I should've known better than to trust her. Patricia had been acting peculiar ever since our reassignment, ever since Frank had come into the picture. Suddenly, there was no affection or excitement, conversation, or effort. Those were the facets of our relationship that she'd accused me of devolving, but was that the case? Was it *my* actions that drove the conspiracy that left me snake-bitten?

Possibly; there was no point in lying to myself about it. A few calculated fabrications wouldn't change the circumstance; my lifecycle is suspended as I float through the universe trapped in a casket. I wasn't perfect but who is? I'd been with the woman for eleven years, what did she expect? We'd screwed each other every which way, through several solar systems I might add, and we'd discussed and debated about every ridiculous topic imaginable.

Sure, I looked at other women, and yeah, I ended up with a bit of a VR porn addiction. Yes, I was tuned out whenever she spoke and occasionally overlooked 'unforgettable' or 'special' dates. My time could have been allocated more reasonably, and sure, I could have offered more thoughtfulness to her. I'd become more inaccessible and spent an inordinate amount of time sequestering myself in less frequented areas of the ship.

I can't fault her for picking up on that but at least I was by myself. I wasn't sleeping around with other crew members.

I'd say I deserved something, a slap in the face or maybe a separation period, but not this well-thought-out hellish uncertainty. Regardless of the caliber of punishment my disinterest merited, the fact that I was completely blindsided shows just how little I actually knew Patricia. The woman I spent the majority of my life with had snapped and premeditated my murder.

As I felt my slow drifting body brush into the coffin's lid-lining I reminded myself that none of it mattered. With or without consent, I'd embarked on a new chapter now. I might as well burn every page before it because it all meant nothing.

The only thing she said to me that truly held relevance anymore were the proud, facetious remarks she made concerning the dosage she'd given me. Was her long-winded explanation the more believable of the two possibilities? How long did I have exactly until my surely agonizing fate? The point of her unsolvable puzzle was to drive me closer toward the madness. To have me adjourned in wonder, immobilized and helpless forever.

Scientifically speaking, I had no idea what she'd put in me or how long it might last. This was obviously a side project she'd been working on for some time now with her fuck buddy. With them leveraging the state-of-the-art technology that was at our disposal, there was no fathomable way to make a hypothesis with zero information on the project or her design.

Based on Patricia's emotional instability, I believe if she had the chance to propel me into a prolonged torture session, she most certainly would jump at the opportunity. That would be her hard target, number one on the long list of violent and painful potential departures she must've constructed. There was an excellent chance she was telling the truth and that I could be bottled in purgatory for a long time.

That word: time. Why does it seem so much more significant now? Probably because I no longer have any sense of it. I don't even know how long I've been in this darkness for, certainly not more than a couple of minutes but who knows? There is simply no way to verify... I'm adrift in the abyss, even if I could find a way to see, I couldn't move. There was no way to track anything. It was simply the exact same moment every second, repeating over and over.

I still have my thoughts at least. My lone form of entertainment... I'd never thought it would come down to this. My existence is barebones, like a fetus with undeveloped eyes. I can still picture things in my head, I can still remember the things I observed before my sight was taken. I can still technically go wherever I want to, whenever I need to... I'll just need to use my imagination more effectively than ever... I'll have to let myself go.

***

The detached and euphoric effects of my drugging had finally worn off. While my heart wasn't physically moving, my mind seemed to believe it was jumping out of my chest. The panic and terror had attached itself and burrowed in like a tick to a deer. The pitch-black bent and contorted, shaping itself; I could feel death close beside me. The slender, boney finger of the shrouded skeleton pointed at me. Two tiny troll-like men beside the Lord of Bones beat their drums hypnotically. I could hear the thunderous blows as they smashed down against the dry-stretched drumskin. Their runny eyes looked like tiny yokes as they glared sinisterly at me. Seconds later, six more appeared, then twelve. They were multiplying.

They'd come for me. How long had it been? If the side effects had worn off, I must have been on the verge of waking up. It shouldn't be long now. Patricia was correct after all; the tension, the dread, and the energy depletion had all found me.

The minuscule teeth of the trolls began to enlarge, the evolution curved their mouths into boomerangs of discontent. They were growing tired of beating those maddening drums, they were anxious to watch their Lord collect me, and then suddenly, they were gone…

I needed to focus strictly on sanity now. Could the outlandishness, that madness that was all I was seeing, be explained? Could it just be the consequences of deep sensory deprivation perhaps? When one is forced into utter isolation without any light cycle, it can lead to strange occurrences. These lengthy periods can easily cause the mind to malfunction, as a student of science that much I'm sure of.

In the absence of information, the human brain still continues to work. It still processes information even if there is nothing there to process. And if there's still nothing, then after a while, it starts to create and fabricate that information itself. Had death physically found me, or was it just a figment brought forth by this extreme seclusion?

I knew what the commonsensical answer was but everything felt so authentic. Like they could reach out and touch me. Not only did I see them as clear as death, but I also heard them. While I couldn't be sure if they were imaginary or not, I had a feeling that I hadn't seen the last of the bizarre dwarfs and the Lord of Bones.

***

I felt the organs inside me begin to tremor like an old engine trying to turn over. Just as the sensation of resurrection overcame me, gravity punched me in the chest and thrust me to the floor of the casket once again. Was my body somehow regaining sensation? How could gravity have returned? The odds that I would drift into another planet so quickly didn't seem realistic... How much time had passed?!

My muddle of thoughts was interrupted by a crashing noise and the sounds of my body knocking around violently in the coffin's interior. Then, just as suddenly as it had found me, the darkness was gone. The lid of my prison must have been torn away in the fall. My sights were ambushed by a florescent flamingo atmosphere that looked to be overrun with trails of amber gasses.

The sky didn't look bright but my eyes still burned having been idle for the unknown duration. The miraculous imagery was overwhelming both physically and emotionally. I took in the warm pink color like I'd never see it again, probably because I'd spent a great deal of thought wondering if I ever would.

I could move again! It didn't even feel like I was controlling it when my body sat up, but I was. Patricia's death sentence had somehow worn off and in a second, seemingly impossible stroke of luck, I'd crash-landed on an inhabitable planet. I was no longer a dead astronaut banished to float on for eternity. I'd been resurrected.

The considerations in my head had momentarily overlapped the spellbinding sights that my pupils were now finally catching up to. There was no way to be certain what covered this new world's surface but the closest thing I could compare it to was a tall fur.

Its hues varied but all within a smoky range, some patches of the fuzz were longer than others and much of the terrain looked slick. A mild wind blew past, causing the surroundings to dance hypnotically.

If someone would've asked me why the bumpy surface disgusted me, I couldn't have told them, it just did. My breathing had accelerated like neither my body nor mind could believe there was actually oxygen to inhale. I rose from the death box and finally mustered the courage to place my bare foot onto the ground. It felt warm and greasy like the inside of a pimple. The fur slipped in between the cracks of my toes as I planted my second foot and tried to avoid slipping.

Some areas of the landscape were more dried out than others, just a few feet away from me sat a generous pile of white decay. I jumped a handful of times doing a 360 but as far as my eyes could see, it was more of the same; endless stretches of the weird furry foot-holding and bleached clay. The idea that I didn't know what lay ahead, and probably wouldn't see it until it was on top of me, was disturbing. I felt directionless based on my initial observations, so I hurdled up over the gray again to take a second look.

Upon second examination, there was one area that was different. The ground was elevated higher like a hill and the zenith appeared to be absent of the fur. Fears of suffering and survival crept into my mind. What would I try to consume first when I got hungry enough? The steaming wet pelt and snowy crust were my only options at the moment. That's when my body started pushing the bushy clumps aside and moving in the direction of the hill. It was the only variance within eyeshot; maybe it offered inhabitable conditions or a less repulsive form of nourishment.

Each step I landed sickened me. I took them slow and deliberately since my balance still felt like it could be thrown off at any minute. The hill was more difficult to scale than it looked, the bare and shiny surface was even oilier than the fuzz. I dug my toes and fingers into the flesh-like incline and literally clawed my way up to the top.

As I hoisted myself to the peak, in the distance I could see it. A triangular hard-shell shape that was elevated by a pair of prickly thin limbs. The shadowy appendages stretched for miles before their pitchfork ends stabbed at their base into the hill. What appeared to be the thing's mouth wasn't merely just an orifice. The intimidating serrated tube also protracted downward and seemed to be both feeding off the hill and serving as a crutch for its alien anatomy. A waterfall of maroon rained down, representing the constant excess of the thing's slurping thirst.

The miscreation's architect clearly had their own unconventional ideas of what life was. What I believed to be its 'eyeball' wasn't housed where one might assume. In fact, it wasn't housed at all. The runny yellowed globe dangled beneath its belly, swinging like a pendulum in the humid breeze—watching. The enormous pupil scanned the surface carefully until it aligned with my path and froze.

An ear-piercing shriek cut loose as the giant began to shiver. The droopy eye retracted into the creature's underbelly and the hind forks pushed its jagged mouth through and into the surface of the planet. The strange lips on the ground parted and swallowed the thing without warning. The floor seemed normal until it began to quake. It rumbled like a stomach that had just taken in a spoiled meal.

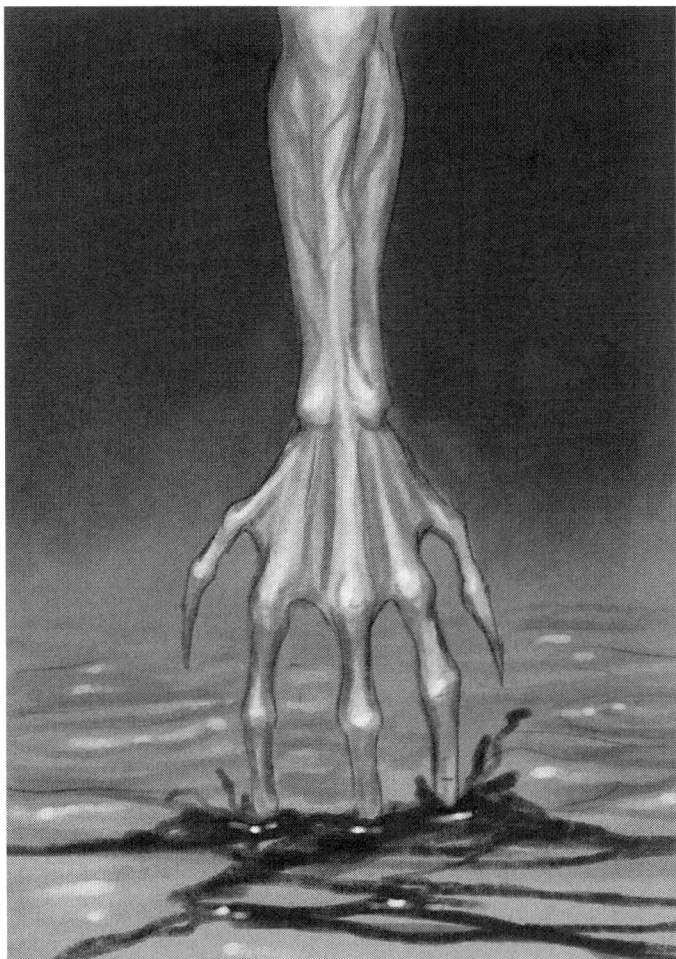

I was terrified by the implications of the shuddering pit but was somehow drawn to it. I don't know why but my instincts screamed me into pursuit. I rushed closer to the cavity, dying to look inside. The rumbles paused momentarily as I neared my toes to the edge. I stuck my neck out but before I could see anything, a strong gust of wind elevated me. Its power was like nothing I'd ever witnessed before. The landscape unexpectedly looked more and more familiar as it raised me further.

With the gust sending me racing back toward space at thousands of feet per second, I observed the shape of the planet now. The further out I was cast, the more the mass of smokey oval fur looked… Human. As the blinding light found me, I was once again immobile. Once my eyes adjusted, I saw the salt and pepper mane covering the back of his greasy skull. It was Sully, our ship's mechanic. His somber expression faced me as he slid off the casket's lid and set it aside.

"Didn't think I'd be seeing you again, buddy. Certainly wasn't hoping to see you like this… But since I didn't get to say goodbye, maybe it's for the best. The least they could've done is given you a good lid, this one was damaged, got you all hung up on exit. You've been snagged up on the purge pod for a while now."

I'd been stuck in the purge pod this whole time? What about the planet I crashed on then? Had the sensory deprivation while I was trapped in exile propelled my voyage of madness? Sully, please! Can you hear me?! I'm not dead! I'M NOT DEAD, Sully! Listen to me!

"Not sure why Patricia didn't invite no one to say goodbye. I know I'm a small fish on a big boat but you were a good guy, Irwin. You deserved to have some words said on your behalf. I'm sure you're in a better place now though, but I'll miss you, brother. I'll see you when I get there."

Sully, don't close the lid! I'm alive, for God's sake, I'm alive still! I know you can hear me; you've got to be able to hear me!

I cried and yelled as best I could while watching him get what I could only assume was a lid that wasn't defective. My muscles were still inoperative, my pleas were useless; he couldn't hear me. Sully said his final goodbyes to me while I felt a strange mixture of dread and excitement ripping my soul in two different directions.

As the new metallic cover slid over me snugly and snuffed out the light, I started to think that things might actually be alright. It didn't matter if he sealed me in for good this time, I'd grown past my confinement. Deep in my soul, I knew that it wouldn't be long until I'd be outside the box again.

MAKING ROOM IN THE BIRDHOUSE

I flew down to the birdbath to get away from them. The vile pond of filth was a collection of dirt and feces. The shallow nutty-looking "water" embodied the disgusting mountains of matter piled within it.

The conditions felt irrelevant, at the moment, because I just needed some space. I'd have killed for a cigarette but that wasn't feasible. I don't know why I kept torturing myself with thoughts from the distant past. Knowing they existed made it more difficult that I didn't have fingers to light one with.

Bace's ashtray was a just across the yard full of half-smoked butts, like a tin bursting with a tar-based tease. The fact that my minuscule birdbrain could still erect these concepts was a torturous miracle. It would have

been a kick in the nuts had I still had some.

Regardless, it was nice to get away for a moment. I was growing weary of watching my younger brother and sister each open their little beaks to whine and beg for Mom's food. The sniveling little shits were taking nourishment from my belly; it was literally ruffling my feathers.

I used the pun often now sadly, there were little means of entertainment in the suddenly crowded birdhouse. These ugly bastards gave me no room to rest nor have a piece of mind. One thing about birds is they never shut the fuck up; silence is a commodity.

Why did Mom have to flash her ass to the first beaked geek that throws a wink her way? She's so desperate the older she gets. It's disgusting really. Now we had two more mouths to account for and countless duties and problems that came with them. She always thinks they'll stay or come back around—what an idiot.

She doesn't have the perspective that I did. When you're a bird, it's not like you don't have wings, you can just hit it and split it. Her wishful thinking bordered on absurd. She just threw her pheasant twat around acting like Prince Charming was there for the long haul. It was better when it was just me, Mom, and the occasional swooning scum vulture who rubbed his cloaca with her; it kept her from going crazy.

I was back at the spot where it all began. Sitting in the disease-riddled puddle when I watched them roll my corpse out of Bace's place. That was the day I said goodbye to the real world, as far as they knew anyway.

It started out just like any other trip, with the three of us watching cartoons. I could feel the fear and adrenaline inside me; we had gone too far this time. I wasn't certain about a whole lot as the vibrant colors melted off of a somehow ominous Buzz Lightyear, but I was POSITIVE something was wrong.

A half-bag of shrooms pulverized into a powder form and guzzled down in a hypnotic mixture of pineapple and orange juice had about knocked my fuckin' socks off already. The handful of nickel-sized peyote buttons were probably still dissolving in my gut. It was about to get worse.

We had done it before though, right? WRONG. Sure, we're psychedelic warriors. Sure, we had broken through to alternate dimensions together before, but my body was telling me—trying to prepare me—that this wasn't the same old song and dance. My body was screaming, and so was Mikey…

I'm not sure why, something about the Lord taking his body for a ride, whatever the fuck that meant. I guess that means he'll cry a whole bunch and open the basement door and scream down the stairs. What in God's name is he yelling at? Or, alternatively, could he be right? Maybe God was inside him piloting his wails?

It was hard to tell with dozens of other eerie voices whispering highly concerning things in my head. I suppose it didn't matter. I turned away from the confusing animation on the tube and tried to block out Mikey's shrieks. Mikey, he didn't like his name and I didn't want to know why.

I glanced over to Bace for guidance, I was melted deep into the cushions of the couch now, helpless. I asked him the only way I could; with my eyes. I begged him to summarize his own theory about Mikey. He ignored me. It wasn't anything intentional, his own befuddlement was spreading him across a canvas of chaos. We knew we were just sitting in his living room but the visuals were too vivid and powerful to deny. The sea creature that had bonded with his lips and chin had gripped him. The slimy sea urchin only allowed him limited freedoms. His crushed aspirations sparkled in his puddled pupils like a galaxy had been imprisoned within them. He was so lost.

The voices bullied me to pry inside him regardless. Telepathically, I felt him and the queerness of the nonsense roaming inside him. Thoughts of linguistic capabilities that I didn't have lurked around every corner of his mind. The elite communication methods were profound. While we could trade ribs using any tongue somehow, he didn't pick up on the fact that my mind and human vehicle were slowly shutting down.

I just wanted to play Super Mario... Maybe watch Duck Tales and have a laugh. The possibility seemed unlikely at this point. Not with that fucking maniac screaming in the basement. Suddenly, I realized he'd moved into the kitchen. The faucet was running faster than Bace's nose down into his beard of tentacles. Why always the tentacles?

I'm not sure how we got there, but we were all of a sudden standing over Mikey while he sat at the kitchen table. He'd been different ever since he decided to display his eyes. There were at least a dozen that had sprouted around his cheeks and forehead. His face was monstrous, but he damn well knew that.

What an asshole. I'm not sure why I was looking in the drawer, but there it was. It rattled and clanged around, calling to me. The pointed sharp silver offered a glimpse at a melting pot of colors. They were telling me to pick up the knife. Pick up the knife and cut those endless fucking eyes out.

Bace felt it, too, but I was grateful that cooler heads prevailed. That's just what the son-of-a-bitch wanted anyway. Why else would he be showing them off like some gaudy rappers' jewelry? He wanted to piss us off, and he was doing a damn good job at it.

I closed the wooden drawer and walked over to the photography displayed on the shelf and pushed it all off. It hit the floor quickly, the glass shattering felt like a great relief. Bace looked at me, his queerness molded into a general rage and confusion.

"What the fuck is wrong with you?" Somehow, he'd found the ability to speak and wonder aloud.

"None of this shit matters? Don't you understand?" The whole time we were communicating flawlessly, then, seemingly out of nowhere, he acted like he didn't understand. "We're fucking dead, don't you get it?! Are you some kind of fucking retard?!"

He was stupefied by my reaction, frozen in time with little sanity to leverage at the moment. I turned the corner into the living room and threw my glasses against the sliding glass door. The stiff connection of glass on glass echoed through the room as I stumbled like a drunken bum down an alley.

"None of it matters you fucking bitch! Mikey! Tell him, Mikey!" I shouldn't have been able to see as clearly as I did with my glasses off.

Mikey crept around the corner and watched over me like an immovable gargoyle. He watched me flail about on the sofa losing my mind. I screamed and dug around in my asshole while he looked upon me with his many eyes of judgment and the deepest repulsion.

"Mikey, you fuckin faggot!" I screamed out. It was over, what else was there left to explain? Why was I still there? Was there a trigger word to finish it off?

"It's like you're in my head, get out of my fuckin' head!" he screamed, banging his palms against his skull. He appeared on the verge of violence or possibly something worse, maybe the verge of truth.

It didn't matter anyway, I was done. I could feel the shock and paralysis. My lungs were slowing and my heart was tired but my soul was the most exhausted of all. I had given up, the voices said it was okay to.

As the rainbow vortex bled around the seams, I stared out through the sliding glass door window. That fucking bird was outside just sitting there in the unmaintained birdbath. The last thing I remembered was thinking I wouldn't bathe in that cesspool if my life depended on it.

Now look at me, I talked a good game but I was full of shit. People think reincarnation is rebirth but it's actually a transfer. I didn't bust out of some egg—I went into an existing creature. Why couldn't there have been a tiger or at least a dog back here?

I must have been a sick man for it to have shaken out how it did. Part of me wanted to believe I'm just still tripping balls right now. Sometimes, when you're in a hallucination fit, it can feel like it's lasting for eternity. But all of this seemed longer than an eternity. I suppose, perhaps, it was a possibility, but it didn't seem likely since things were still evolving around me.

Bace suddenly poked his depressed face out back for a smoke before he left for work. His shirt was tight enough to see that he didn't have nipple rings anymore; that in itself was evidence of change. He also got a new tattoo across his throat that said "Pisstaind Shirt" (the name of our old band). The balls on that kid; who the fuck walks around with the word *piss* on their neck? Band or not, dead friend or not, it didn't seem appropriate for a man of his tier of normalcy.

The boys at the shop must have thought he went fucking crackers. He certainly looked a bit off each day that drove the present away from my overdose or heart attack. I'm not sure how I died but I consider myself fortunate; I was able to die around people I loved. While the life had been sucked out of me, it was clear that I wasn't the only one.

I saw a bottomless sadness worming through him as he pulled a deep drag on the Newport short. I wish I could just tell him it will be okay. I wish I could just have one more conversation with him and let him know how good the run we had really was. While much of the fondness and nostalgia that surrounded our friendship was predicated in drug use, we knew damn-well it was so much more than that.

He seemed more reclusive since I'd been watching him. I hadn't seen Mikey stop by in some time either. Maybe he was just too into his business? I doubt it, but it was possible. The likely reason for his absence was, in some ways, probably because they blamed themselves (or each other) for my untimely end. I wish I could tell them it wasn't their fault. I wish I could tell them to hang out again.

I wish Bace would feed us some fuckin' bird seeds. Just fill-up the feeder for one day even! I know he's unmotivated and still in the dark but I'm getting tired of killing those lawn toads and chewing up their guts only to spit them into the jaws of my brethren. Look at him, just like before, eating sunflower seeds all the time, and not leaving a kernel behind. Cheap fuck.

I swear I'm gonna kill one of those birds if things don't get better around here. If there was only a way to get away, to get past this nightmarish madness.

Wait... That's it. I've gotta get them back together. If I can just get them around each other again... If they could trip, I know it would bring them out of this funk. How the fuck could I do that though?

Suddenly, it came to me like a glorious epiphany. It's like a higher power cooked up the entire plot for me. There were a few steps involved that I would need to complete. I couldn't believe that I hadn't thought of it before. It was most likely my pea-sized brain that had hindered me, but this glaring premonition that was gifted to me felt like fate. I might be a bird now but I still have abilities, some that make our connection a possibility. Forget hunting for worms today... I'm hunting for SHROOMS.

I hadn't scored any in ages and even when I was in my human form, snagging an ounce was like winning the fuckin' lottery. We were lucky to get a batch or two a year. But this was preordained; something would lead me to them today.

A feeling inside guided me down toward downtown Providence. My dark wings sliced through the gray city smog poetically, it couldn't weigh me down any longer—nothing could. I got down to Thayer Street, keeping my eyes peeled for the stoner bongs shops I remembered from a lifetime ago.

I slowed down and perched myself atop a coffee shop across the road from an establishment called "Ethnic Concepts." The mustard and plum exterior of the shop called to me. Those hippie fuckers would be all over this place like stink on shit. They'd be picking up their patchouli and pipes, readying themselves to go home and get laced.

A lanky white fella with a tie-dye T-shirt and crusty blonde dreads leaking from his Marley beanie entered.

He was accompanied by a skateboarding figure dressed in all-black wearing a hoodie. No one seemed to come out for some time. I was getting a little bored waiting, so I keyed in on some college cunt.

I overheard her talking shit about one of her alleged "friends." I knew her type all too well. A real vindictive backstabber and proud of it. I hovered a few feet over her pristine, methodically-styled mane and dropped a big wet shit on her head. She hollered and cursed me but there ain't much you can do when a bird takes a dump on you. She's lucky I didn't aim for the mouth.

Suddenly, the jingling door of Ethnic Concepts swung open and the gnarly hippie and his shadowy companion headed up the street. I played it cool sailing high above their heads avoiding detection. Not that they would be on the lookout for an incognito bird anyway, but it was just for good measure.

A few streets over, they slowed at the doorway of a college townhouse. They lazily ascended the steps of the building while I watched and landed on the edge of a crumbling plant holder that hung just outside their room. The dying cannabis plant in the dry dirt was a further indicator that they might have what I needed.

The gloomy figure finally removed the hoodie along with the rest of the clothes that covered their body. While the skater on the street gave off more of a dudish aura, on closer inspection, it was, in fact, a sporty chick... And she was a fuckin' smoke-show.

I hadn't seen a pussy in ages, even her overly hairy, bolt-pierced sagging lips looked appeasing somehow. The hippie had a real strange dick; it curved like a horseshoe and it appeared he'd been gifted with extra foreskin. The lumpy white cheese that encrusted it was about the last thing I'd hoped to encounter...

I was getting too distracted by these scrubs having their gross sex. My mind resettled on the task at hand. I needed the shrooms.

I scanned the filthy room through the rubbish until my beady eyeballs landed on the Jamaican cracker's desk. That's why I'd been drawn to him; he had a stash that made him look like he partied with Steve-O before he got clean.

"Open up the fuckin' window, it's hot in here," the scum-skank whined as they switched positions.

The haggard hippie slid the window open and I remained out of his sights; a higher force was in play here. Part of me wanted to take some of the heroin and crack that was there too, but I knew that was foolish. If this was gonna work, we had to do it right. My focus had to be on acquiring the poisonous mushrooms.

I was done listening to his shitty jam band in the background while he got his dick wet. Thankfully, they screwed loud enough to allow me in and out quickly but not flawlessly. One of my flapping wings knocked over a dolphin-shaped bong that shattered on the floor. As I scurried to the open window, the smell of year-old bong water invaded me. I made it away with the bag of shrooms sealed securely in my beak to the dismay of the sexually interrupted.

When I returned to Bace's house, I hid the shrooms in the shed. I didn't want any hairy animals (including him) stumbling across the temptation before it was time. Afterward, I looked in the window of his house to check on him. He was in the bathroom struggling to shave his back. He tried to stretch his stubby but diesel arms behind himself to no avail. After a while, he just wiped the mass of shaving cream off his spine with a towel and went to bed as a sadness sunk into his eyes.

I followed his lead and flew off to get some shuteye, too. If I was going to finish up my prep to reunite us, I would need to be rested for tomorrow. I went back to the birdhouse where my screeching brother and sister were fast asleep. Momma was away, probably fuckin' some trashy bird again. It wasn't uncommon for her to disappear for days and leave me to advocate for our family.

It was just as I had about found the sandman when they started up. Squawking and pleading for a midnight snack. Their grainy faces were still stained with blood from the toad bellies they'd feasted on earlier. I tried to warn them but they wouldn't listen. They didn't realize how important tomorrow was. I needed my rest and they were in no mood to afford it to me.

I vaulted forward and shoved the acute point of my beak repeatedly through my young brother's soft, developing skull. In a strange effort to offer him understanding, I'd robbed him of the ability to think and blood oozed from the portal I'd gored into his psyche. He was quiet, but little sister was screaming now. I'd give her something to scream about for once.

I'd seen mom fuck those nomadic birds in the past, rubbing my cloaca wasn't going to do the trick to shut her up. I bowled her over, rushing forward with the ferocity and hunger of a linebacker angling at the passer. Feathers flew out as I drove my beak into her cavity. It tasted of shit and rotten toad as I reamed her out further. I didn't stop the pecking until I could fit my entire head within the gash I'd created. With my face covered in blood and bird shit, I could finally get some rest.

I don't know what drove me over the edge, I can't say it was anything more than the unending racket and lack of space. I pushed the desecrated nest with their corpses out of the birdhouse and took my old spot from before they existed. As I slowly drifted into sleep, I couldn't help but think that what I'd done wasn't just killing birds. No matter how I drew it up, I'd killed my equals. At least in that moment…

***

The next morning, I looked out the window of the birdhouse and could see Bace examining the defiled nest and slaughtered birds on the ground below. He looked like he wasn't quite sure what to think about it as he dragged a deep cloud of menthol into his lungs. I could smell the smoke; it was the closest thing I could get to a cig at the time, so I enjoyed it dearly. I would have enjoyed it even more if it wasn't being severely molested by his morning breath. I wish he brushed his teeth prior, but beggars can't be choosers.

"What the?" He engaged in a squatting position and

examined their wounds closer. "Some sick shit going on out here…" he mumbled to himself.

He put the Newport out in the birdbath like a true classless asshole. There he was acting like he shed a tear for the birds, then he pollutes the entire water supply. I wasn't sure if it was ignorance, laziness, or stupidity. Knowing Bace, all three were at play.

I spied on him as he got into his car and picked his nose. He started the engine and drove his finger deep. It reminded me of when I was digging around in my ass just before I died. The urgency felt real, but my path felt clear like there was no other road to take.

As he drove away, I knew I needed to find a way to enter the house. I flapped my wings and examined the house's exterior for vulnerabilities. I could see through the bathroom window where he'd left it cracked halfway, and furthermore, the door inside that led to the house was open! The only thing that was separating me from getting inside was a thin layer of screen. This would be a piece of cake!

As I approached the mesh, I noticed that wasn't the only thing stopping me. He must have left the window and door open because he just finished dropping his morning deuce. Christ, did he have Indian food? I hadn't smelled a scent that daunting since… Well since I had my beak up my sister's ass the prior evening.

After giving it a few minutes for the potent stench to clear out, I easily pecked my way through the screen. I fluttered noisily around the house, searching for an appropriate picture. After rummaging through some of the more frequently used rooms and coming up empty-handed, I made my way upstairs. Maybe his music room would hold the key? I noticed there were some of our classic outdated instruments that we used at our shitty shows ages ago. Also, some retro video games, sneaker boxes, and other randomness. Then, suddenly, I saw it: the HIV Boys picture.

If anything could stir up memories of the "good old days," this would be it. It was a photo that we'd all taken on Halloween years ago. Mikey was dressed like Chris Redfield and I was an old man. Ironically, a form I'd never been able to progress to in my own life. Bace was dressed lazily as a character from The Walking Dead, not sure which one because I never watched the show. It basically consisted of a black hat, black shirt, and jeans. We referred to the photo as the HIV Boys because we were all standing idiotically against the chipped brick wall of a longstanding factory across the street from one of his brother, Jose's, legendary house parties. The gigantic letters *HIV* just happened to be spray-painted behind us. Classy area.

As I thought about the comical memory, I recalled a rich sensation of what it was like to be human again. The privilege I'd so casually enjoyed without stopping to think how lovely it could be on some nights. The enlightenment brought a tear to my eye.

I set the wistfulness aside and began to violently bang my beak into the glass as though what laid on the other side was everything I'd been waiting for. I couldn't crack it. It was a quality frame I suppose. I decided to see if gravity would do the right thing for us and, just like my siblings the night prior, I nudged the stylish frame off the desk.

It broke in a manner that my destiny saw fit; splitting down the middle like a sandwich being pulled apart. The image was now mine for the taking. I folded it once over as best I could and pinned it firmly between my jaws. I had no choice but to leave the mess as is and made my way back out through the section of screen where I'd initially infiltrated the premises.

Last I remembered, Mikey still lived in Attleboro. It used to be about a forty-minute drive back when I could operate a motor vehicle. Via flight, it probably would cut that time in half as I didn't have to obey the rules of the road—I was literally above all else.

Flying was the best part about being a bird, that and the lawlessness. Things were so much simpler this way. Not that I condone killing or anything, but sometimes a murder was necessary. There were no courts, no doctor check-ups, no worries really. Just annoyances. It seemed like it was all up to karma for the most part and that was a system I could dig. Although I did savagely slay those birds the night prior…

I tried to move on from those thoughts; I'm not sure exactly what got into me. It kind of felt like that moment during my trip where I considered cutting out Mikey's eyeballs. I was able to stunt that action, but for some reason, slaughtering the birds was unavoidable.

As I closed in on Mikey's modest neighborhood, I couldn't figure out why this was the first time I'd really ventured out. Until my abrupt enlightenment, I'd never even thought about visiting anyone. I didn't even know I had the capability. It's like my pellet-sized command center was restricted from thinking about it. Instead, I was wrapped up in caring for those fucking birds. Now that I realized I could've done it all along, I felt guilty for not seeing any of them. My real human mother and stepfather, I missed them so much. I'd been left in that foul birdhouse with an incredible void. A gaping void created not only by my bottomless adoration for them but also for my sweet and beautiful wife, Katherine.

They'd probably be pretty jerked if they knew I

could've done so and neglected to. But what would I say? I couldn't speak with them, I couldn't laugh with them, I couldn't hug or kiss them. They wouldn't even know it was me. I suppose no choice was the right one.

I was in the general vicinity of his last known residence now; I could feel it. *What was the name of that damn street? Oakland! Of course!* The irony was he followed the Raiders and had found himself there, if not for that, I'm not sure I would've remembered.

As I settled on the fire escape outside of Mikey's third story apartment, I knew getting into this place would probably be a little trickier. Or I could just go in through the open window?! A distantly familiar ritual leaked out the oblong opening; he was in the shower. Thankfully, I'd caught him before work, what timing!

As I closed in, I heard the streaming sounds of a strong showerhead and lathered soap rubbing against his massive frame. He had quite a bit to wash so I should have enough time to pull it off. In addition to the steamy resonances, Mikey sang the sad songs of his past. His smokey tinge wailed without regard, bouncing off the turquoise shower tiles like a man in pain, like a lost soul. *Was he crying?*

While his state distressed me deeply, I still had this feeling like there might be hope. But I knew for me to have any chance of amending things, I had to get the bait to and from the big bastard.

He drifted further into hysteria as I dropped in smoothly, dipping under the barrier's opening and over the shower curtain to the other side. I'd managed to stay clear of the water and Mikey didn't know the half of it. He still leaned against the tile, head pressed into his elbow, sobbing like a man-child.

Does he just cry like this every morning? Seems weird but

also like him. I'd seen him break down on trips in the past, releasing the raw emotion without a second thought. That was exactly what trippin' was for, this sort of therapeutic purge; a deep and shadowy spiritual cleansing. But outside of those profound experiences, I'd always pictured him as one that held it together.

Before I could agree if I believed in my internal ponderance or not, I saw it: his neatly-folded work uniform and the keys to his rig. I laid the HIV Boys photo over the giant's garb he called clothing and opened it up as best I could. It was positioned in a way that he should be faced with it as he exited the wash box.

I took the keyring in my mouth and bit down as hard as I could. If I dropped these, it was all over. This had to be executed to perfection to pull it off the way I envisioned. I fluttered my black wings strategically, elevating my bird frame back over the running shower. The silly prick was still in a messy heap, and just as I bolted through the window, I shitted all over the back of his head. I owed him that much. I only wished I could have seen the expression on his face when I let it rain all over him.

It wasn't that bad; he was in the shower and could shampoo it right out of his hair, yet part of me hoped he missed a clump of the milky-slick turd. As I glided through the air, my jaw ached from the weight of the keys. I needed to return to Bace's house at once.

***

By the time Mikey arrived at Bace's house, I'd already pecked a hole into the central air ductwork where I'd also stashed the shrooms. That would allow me to move about the house into any area I desired and listen to them converse. I set Mikey's keyring down on the kitchen counter and finally made my way back outside.

He couldn't drive his rig without a key so he was sitting in the driveway stuffed into his Isuzu Amigo looking impatient. Just as I'd suspected he would, Mikey took the bait. Finding the picture in lieu of where his keys should have been presented only one option as to what could've happened. There was simply no one else it could have been.

I watched intently as, finally, Bace pulled into the driveway in his faded Bonneville. The tires immediately seized up when he saw whose car it was, as if he was about to be forced into a conversation that he was anything but prepared for.

Eventually, the wheels started to turn again, and the car rolled along, parking beside Mikey. Bace's brow was crinkled, a fresh coat of the old "what the fuck" expression painted all over him.

They withdrew from their vehicles simultaneously, each waiting for the other to say something. I could tell that Mikey felt like it was on Bace to break the silence since he believed he'd broken into his apartment somehow. On the other hand, Bace had no clue he was thinking that. As far as he knew, Mikey had just randomly been waiting in his driveway for who-knows-why or how long. This was all after being a ghost for a stretch of time I couldn't even calculate.

"Well?" Mikey asked, extending the olive branch in his own oafish way.

"Well, what?" Bace replied candidly.

"C'mon…"

Bace's gaze of confusion was solid and authentic as the words he spoke. "Why are you here?"

"Why am I here? You took the keys to my truck guy, don't play stupid. I had to call out of work today, you could've just told me if you wanted to see me."

"I have no earthly idea what you're talking about."

Mikey fished around in his pocket a bit before removing the picture. As he unfolded it, a warm feeling came over Bace. The still image from years past generated a grin on his face. It was clear as I observed him that he hadn't smiled like that in some time.

"I thought I was the only one that had that picture," Bace stated curiously.

"You are, so why'd you leave it in my bathroom?"

"Bro, what are you talking about? I was at work all day, I haven't been to your dirty-ass house since… Since… You know."

"Well, how is it possible then?" Mikey's patience was beginning to wear thin. I could tell he was starting to feel like he was being fucked with.

"Dude, just come inside, we'll go to the room where the picture is and I'll show you that I didn't fuckin' do it, okay?"

I scurried back into the ventilation system as quietly as possible, beating them back inside. I got a look at them through the gridded steel above the stove from a bird's eye view.

Bace unlocked the door and set his lunch bag down in the kitchen. "Fuckin' racist, always blame the black guy," he muttered under his breath.

Mikey ignored his playful jest and approached the marble counter as he'd done countless times before. His keys jumped out from the piles of junk that littered the unkempt countertop. The Blue Rhino logo and cartoon animal attached to it were just too enjoyable not to look at.

"So, you weren't at my house, huh?" he quipped, pointing toward the ring.

"I'm so confused…" I could see his curiosity was bubbling trying to make sense of it. He stepped over to the broom closet and removed the black aluminum bat and held it firmly. "Come upstairs with me."

Mikey saw that his demeanor had grown serious, something definitely had him shook up. I watched the goosebumps rise upon their flesh. To me, it was funny. They probably thought some madman was lurking inside at this point.

I was able to make my way through the air duct and reached the room before they had finished creeping up the stairs. The vent I stared through in the music room was almost directly above the destroyed frame that contained the HIV Boys photo prior.

I could see Bace's black and white Ewing's find the hardwood floor below first. Once they were able to confirm there was no threat in the room, their focus turned to the damaged home good.

Bace picked it off the floor, twisting and examining it. "Someone was in my house today…"

"Yeah, welcome to my world. So, it really wasn't you then?"

Bace shook his head, offering a speechless response, his frightened look said all that was required. "I need a beer," he said, setting the frame back on the desk before heading back downstairs.

I could hear them opening a couple of bottles of brew in the kitchen until they eventually migrated to the living room: the last place we had all been together. I retrieved the shrooms from the stash spot and headed over to the vent above the couch to join them. I felt like there would be a sign for when the time was right.

I would just know.

They each resumed their seats on the couch, just like before, but there was a glaring void on the sofa without me squished in between. I could see them each somberly guzzling down their beers, neither wanted to acknowledge the elephant (or in this case, the bird) in the room. Little did they know I was right there with them, ready to make things magical again.

"So, what the fuck is going on?" Mikey asked.

Bace paused from his chugging and let out a guttural burp, "Honestly, I don't even give a fuck. Whatever mystery is there can just be there."

The two continued drinking in an awkward silence that Bace didn't intend to create. There was too much going on, things needed to slow down. He brought it back to basics, "So, how you been?"

"I'm aight, I guess. You?" Mikey followed up.

"Yeah. Sure do miss him though."

"Yeah me, too, man, me too. Fuckin' miss trippin' with that crazy fucker even more, despite him digging around in his ass." He managed to score a minimal chuckle out of Bace before continuing, "Even though it turned out the way it did, there's a part of me that wouldn't change the things we been through together for anything."

"He went too far that day, we all went too far that day." Bace lit up a cigarette uncharacteristically; the stress that infested his brain was consuming him.

"It's just fuckin' sad, I feel like we still had so many journeys to take, so much more shit to learn and understand," Mikey polished off his bottle and reached for one of the many they'd lugged over.

"You know he almost fuckin' killed you that night?" Bace confessed, taking a drag that killed a quarter of the Newport.

"How do you know?" Mikey asked, unsure if he should believe him.

"Because I felt it. Do you remember what we wrote on that paper? *WE ARE OK.* Man, were we fuckin wrong."

"Should have known that was a buttload of false hope."

"Yeah, it should be obvious. If you ever have to write down that you're okay, it's safe to say that you're not fuckin' okay."

They both enjoyed a moment of laughter that died out quickly. Bace looked over at Mikey as a glossiness coated his bloodshot eyes. The water was welling up like I'd seen in the shower that morning.

"I feel like I'm about to be the one to kill something lately. I got all this… This… Pent-up anguish, this horror, and negativity stewing inside me. I'm a fuckin' mess. It's a constant rerun; every day, the mess gets bigger and bigger. I keep telling myself one more trip could fix it all, get that euphoria slipping back out of my skin, but I feel guilty…"

"So, you still haven't?"

"Nah, why, have you?"

"Nope, I haven't had the balls to even attempt to sniff any out. I just find myself alone on this couch, the same furniture he died on, thinking that I might be better off dead, too. All I do is drink and think."

"Fuck it, maybe we should just trip together again," Mikey finally put it out there, an idea that had been stewing in his mind since the day I died. Undoubtedly, he was fantasizing about it while sitting in the driveway all afternoon. Perhaps he'd also been judiciously choreographing the best means to sprinkle it into the unavoidable conversation from the moment he knew it was going to happen. It was the moment that I'd been waiting for.

I removed a pair of big nasty caps from the bag and set them on the inside of the aluminum duct, then carefully wrapped the baggie in a manner where it shouldn't spill out. I pushed it through the vent with my beak and held my breath, standing out of eyeshot.

I could hear their initial concern rapidly evaporate, then their confusion. Finally, excitement was up to bat and stay for the rest of the night. They tore into the baggie like savages. It could have come from the Devil himself and those two would still have been munching away, no problem.

After a minor inspection, they decided not to question the miracle. They weren't focused on how or why things were happening they were just enjoying the ride. To them, some unknown force had arranged their togetherness and then gifted them an offering. Fuck everything else.

I was ingesting the last crumbles of my caps as they returned with a coffee bean grinder full of brown hallucinogenic powder. This was an old trick; in fact, it was the same one we'd used the day I died. Grinding it to fine dust helped the poison enter your system almost immediately. As they dumped the foul fungus into two glasses, they mixed it in with some beer. Then, in harmony, they both washed back the nastiness with a separate, refreshing chaser wave of beer that cleansed their taste buds. And now we waited…

I'm not sure if it was because of the weight and dimensions of my physique, but that shit hit me almost immediately. If they weren't already there beside me, they weren't far behind.

My feathers, beak, and everything else broke down from their solid form until I was a russet goop-like substance dangling from the vent above them. It was poetic how my inner slime made its way down to the exact spot where I died. I piled up higher and higher, I had a very distinct feeling that I was now somehow much bigger than the body that I had melted down from. As I began to form an outline, I was nervous. My eyeballs surfed through the gunk mound as it erected and I caught a glimpse of my reflection in the mirror hanging on Bace's wall beside the fireplace.

I looked alien-like; some interplanetary space filth that crash-landed at the beginning of a double feature drive-in movie. Somehow, Bace and Mikey were at peace as if what they were seeing was exactly what they'd been expecting; just another stroll in the park.

As I slowly took form, the figure I was summoned as occupied about the same amount of space that my body could have when I was human, except there was nothing human about me anymore.

While my body was proportionate, my head was much larger and still that of a bird. My drippy distorted beak came to a sharp intimidating point, and my eyes were filled with a cyclone of madness. My shape was similar; I had arms, legs, and a cock again but my endless feathers were spiraled and pushed out from all my reformed human extremities. It felt like both of the realities I'd participated in had somehow overlapped.

Everyone was too shell-shocked to speak. At first, it was fine but now it felt awkward. We could easily converse telepathically but it seemed weird. Why couldn't I at least have pants? That surely didn't help. The unavoidable grumblings of many voices, which weren't our own, were interrupted by a knock at the sliding glass door.

Bace turned white and wide-eyed like he'd seen a poltergeist. The scene just past the glass more than warranted the reaction; the impossible had found me. My brother and sister, now in a form similar to mine, had somehow found life again.

Their bodies were still dismantled in the way I'd left them. My bro's skull crushed from the pecks of my warped beak and my sissy's rear reamed out, still leaking all the blood and shit one could imagine.

I was horrified, I felt like my dirty secret had arrived to be revealed in front of my closest friends. While we were unable to speak, they both knew it was me, for Christ sake, it was my spot on the couch. The weight of the situation left little opportunity to discuss anything or offer our greetings.

They knocked again with their rotten whiney beaks, but this time, more aggressively. They knocked so hard that it sent the message if you don't let us in—we'll just come in.

Bace looked at us filled with fear but ready to speak, "Should I let them in?"

He sounded so nonchalant to me; I'm not sure who he was trying to convince. Neither Mike nor I could offer an answer. I desperately wanted to say no, but I was shackled by my own cynicism. Whether he let them in or not, they were going to come in, therefore, I remained idle.

Somehow, he found the energy to control the drugs and stand on two feet. He waddled over to the sliding glass and pushed it open.

"Hey… So… What's up? How can I help you guys?"

My brother placed his palm against his forehead and slowly controlled Bace's direction. My sister opened her blown-out undercarriage and readied herself. My brother deliberately pushed Bace's entire skull inside her gruesome cavern until it was inserted completely.

Flashes shot into our joint consciousness all at once; we saw the vulgar atrocity that I had committed in cold bird-blood. We watched what felt like endless pecks to their young, disfigured shells until the damage was irreparable. As the young birds in the vision became unrecognizable, my distorted beak and manic actions became all the clearer. I was a monster.

The whispering chirps of the feathered youth took the place of all the other voices within us. Mikey and I remained immobile on the couch as Bace's head was drawn back out of my sister's raspberry chute. He turned back to the kitchen, cheeks covered in the vomit-inducing concoction, and took hold of the bat.

He beat Mikey first, turning his neck black and purple before caving in his head. It looked like a sloppy buffet plate; a mixture of hamburger and pie filling carelessly stacked on top of each other by some slob. I felt his consciousness ripping away from the group, he was fucking dead.

I only wished that Bace finished me that easily. It seemed that he'd played out my brother's murder on Mikey, so now he was set to orchestrate my sister's sodomization and slaughter upon me. He beat my legs, hips, and cock until I had no feeling. Until they were just a crumpled heap of overly tenderized meat and fragmented bone.

He expelled so much sweat, he looked like he was losing weight. He took his shirt off and his caramel skin glistened. He still didn't have the nipple rings but the bushy cabbage patch of back hair slithered about him like thousands of daddy-long-legs.

He bent me over and positioned me for his next assault. It didn't take him long to work one of the empty beer bottles half-way into my rectum. He'd clearly been hitting the weights again as he placed it in with ease like setting a golf ball down on a tee. He swung with a herculean might, his biceps bulging as the aluminum crushed the green, glass into a thousand pieces. The cutting dust and particles ripped into my anal gristle destructively, slicing it all to shit.

My pulsating sphincter was secreting liquified feces, blood, and hunks of pink flesh as he inserted the second bottle. If that first one felt like a home run, the next one was a grand slam. My ass felt like a sick black hole of violence and destruction. I stopped being able to feel, I could sense myself slipping away again. It was similar to the first time that I died but with an extra helping of excruciating agony.

***

Hell wasn't the absolute worst place to be. After the whole reincarnation bit, I honestly thought it'd be back to that, but strangely that wasn't the case. It was difficult to explain or make sense of any of it, so we simply didn't try to. It got old rather quickly and we had other things to talk about. We just took it for what it was and tried not to complain too much.

I say "we" because it didn't take me long to find Mikey, he was there too. I always assumed if there was an afterlife that we'd revert back to a complete version of ourselves. That wasn't the case in hell at least. However you went out, is exactly how you came in. And while there were a bunch of assholes walking around with fucked up grills, Mikey was tall enough to pick out from the crowd eventually. I had no idea how long it had taken me but in time, I'd found him.

I was still the extreme reamed-out bird-human hybrid version of myself. My ass never stopped leaking and it was nearly impossible for me to have a bowel movement. It sucked but at least I found Mikey who had taught himself this kind of retarded version of sign language that he made up to communicate with me since he couldn't speak.

Not too long after me and Mikey linked up, we found Bace, too. He was the most intact of us all. He got locked up after murdering us and sodomizing me. He told us his time on Earth finished up with a bedsheet around his neck on death row. He was a little pale with some bruising on the throat but aside from that, he looked like a hundred bucks.

The more I thought about the circumstance, the fact that Bace and I had both found the inferno seemed appropriate. I'd murdered those two birds in the form of a bird, which is just like killing people. Bace reenacted that sequence with people, which *is* killing people…

What the fuck was Mikey doing with us though? I'd never actually seen him do anything evil or plot anything sinister. That motherfucker must have had some major skeletons in the closet; jumbo shrimp status. Bace and I tried to ask him about it but his "sign-language" was undecipherable. It was hard to tell if he was bullshitting us. With his head mutilated in the bizarre fashion that it was, he was essentially incapable of transmitting an expression any longer. When he was happy, hungry, sad, excited, or tired, he still just looked like a pile of beat-up meat.

I suppose it didn't matter anyway; it was just like with the bird hierarchy here—no court of appeals to be found anywhere in this bitch. When you took it all apart every which way possible and put it back together just as many times, it boiled down to one of those old choose-your-own-adventure books. There were only three possible conclusions that were feasible enough to consider:

1. Mikey was either a closeted sadist, perpetuating a façade that disguised his horrific deeds like a masterful illusionist.

OR

2. Mikey had been the unfortunate victim of both murder and a dogmatic blunder of cosmic proportions.

OR

3. We were all *still* tripping…

AWFUL THINGS

Miles had an unknown skin condition that caused widespread plum-colored splotches to cover most of his body. In fact, his entire head was shaded violet save for an ear and a half-dollar-sized runny hexagon patch that sat uncentered on his forehead. His mother told him that his skin was beautiful but the world seemed to feel differently.

During his painful stretch in the school system, Miles was unable to socially evolve. Embarrassed about who he was, he'd been confined to a suffocating shy box. The ones who he learned with would rather whisper unpleasantries behind his back than see what potential lay beyond the flesh. Society's deep-rooted cruelty forced Miles to keep his distance; not just from them but from nearly anyone.

His father's abandonment diseased his confidence as a man. Instead, he grew quite accustomed to living a simple, lonesome, and unfulfilling life.

Before he knew it, school was over and everyone he never knew had found jobs and disappeared into obscurity. His own job was a lot like school had been; there was no one to confide in and his peers all came off very snake-like. The streak of isolation continued. He felt alone in most respects but at least he still had his mom. She was the only person that had ever been able to make him smile. She shared her love with all of her heart like a warm ray of sunshine. She nurtured him unconditionally and made him feel the love that all the others kept from him. She was his everything until his everything was no more...

As she got older, Miles stayed close to her, wanting to ensure that she was always comfortable and cared for. She could still fend for herself just fine but Miles liked to go out of his way to make things easier for his mother. After work, he fixed her dinner and cleaned the house. Then he set the television to her favorite shows while she laughed and ate her supper. It was a simple, uneventful life but they were both grateful they had each other.

One day while at work, Miles received a phone call. It was unusual for him to get a call there; his intestines immediately began to tremble. The gruff male voice that spoke on the phone first confirmed his identity, then he explained to Miles that his mother was dead. Witnesses to the tragedy verified that she had suddenly jumped in front of a bus downtown that was passing her at full speed. Without any warning, she was gone, and she was never coming back.

A sickening despondency and morbid curiosity traded blows inside him. He had to know more about what happened, no matter how stomach-churning the specifics of her demise might be. He made his way to the police station and found the gruesome information readily available in a lengthy report.

They described how her body exploded all over the bus's oversized square front windows, horrifying its many passengers. How she came from out of nowhere and then, moments later got sucked down under the huge tires. They were still trying to move forward a few seconds before the bus driver realized the horror that was unfolding.

During that time, the ruthless rubber pulverized her into a misshapen mess of humanity (it wasn't surprising considering the undertaker only agreed to take the job if he granted a closed casket service). When the beastly vehicle finally slowed, her twisted frame was a big part of the reason; what was left of Mom's fragmented corpse sat sandwiched in between the two rear wheels.

The bone-breaking gridlock squeezed the essence and innards from within her like ringing out a rag until it was nearly dry.

Miles couldn't make a lick of sense of the mayhem. They were calling it a suicide but that conclusion seemed absurd. They all said she took her life willingly but he just couldn't believe that. They didn't know her, only he did. She seemed perfectly content with the life they led. She wouldn't just leave him behind. She wouldn't just suddenly off herself in nauseating fashion without saying anything to him, would she?

The mystery was the only thing left in his life with any meaning or relevance now that she was gone. He needed to know why she did it. It began to feast on him, eating away like he was riddled with hundreds of tiny famished parasites. His own thoughts became his worst enemy.

Miles never snooped around before; he never had a reason to. Everything was fine or at least appeared that way astatically. It felt strange looking through his mother's belongings. The sensation of embarrassment seemed silly since one typically needed other people in the equation for the feeling to actually occur. He didn't have a choice though, there was simply nothing else he could do but search. He turned the entire house upside down, tearing through every crevice like a madman looking for a crumb. Nothing of significance surfaced until his shaking hand reached under her bed.

After pushing aside mounds of clutter that mainly consisted of dusty nostalgic clothing and old faded shoeboxes, his skin touched against a texture that was different than the rest of the mess walled up under her sleeping space. With the bed being pressed against the wall, it seemed reasonable to think that this item had been strategically displaced.

Miles extracted a quaint wooden box that looked older than him. The weird container had the word "THINGS" carved onto the top of it. In his mind, he had no doubt that it had been hidden from him. His mother did not want him to see whatever was inside the box. Holding such an intimate possession felt dirty. He held his oxygen and opened the hood of the box.

Inside, there was a folded square of paper taped to the roof with the name "Miles" written on it, and at the bottom of the box sat countless crumpled notes. For an unknown reason, the balled papers called to him more so than the note that was clearly addressed to him. He took hold of the first one and carefully unraveled it. The paper read: Disfigure your child.

Miles's eyelids grew wide, he looked back at the mirror standing in the room's corner at his hideous eggplant exterior. What did it mean?

"This is some kind of sick joke…" he whispered to himself while reaching for the next paper. He unfolded the next paper quicker than the first: Sodomize a man.

He didn't stop, he went to the next: Burn a church.

Then the next: Kiss a dead body.

Followed by: Eat human flesh.

He couldn't stop, mainly because he didn't want to pause and think about what he'd already seen actually meant. These were not just "Things," these were awful, despicable things the likes of which he didn't believe his mother was even capable of thinking.

The next one made him stop dead in his tracks, it struck him so profoundly that he had no choice in the matter. "Murder your husband" were the next words revealed in the scribbly black ink that was unmistakably his mother's handwriting.

These things couldn't be true; she always told him that his father had left them behind. Miles always assumed he'd been bastardized by his father's actions, that's what he was told. Were these notes telling a different story now?

Why was there a box of awful things under his mother's bed? Was this how she blew off steam? Could it have simply been ideas that she never acted on? Or, most troublesome of all, had she actually done these awful things? She simply wasn't there to answer the question, he could only hope her note to him could make sense of it. He removed the tack that pinned it to the hood of the box and unfolded the note. It read:

My Dearest Miles,

If you are reading this then you've have come across my box of secrets. I didn't hide the box in a difficult place because I wanted you to find it—you deserved to find it. If you decided to read the "Things" in this box before my letter, you may be confused, so this letter will hopefully make a little more sense of them. I know the words and acts portrayed must be shocking. I cannot lie to you from beyond the grave as I did for your entire life. Every one of them is something that I did… Or maybe a better phrasing would be that I allowed to be done. But these aren't things I did for myself; they are things I did for humanity as a whole.

For some time, my life in many ways was very much like yours, my dear sweet Son; fruitless and painful. Companionship and glee were always elusive. I had your father, of course, but not much else. He was a good man but we differed in many ways. He was not fond of the outdoors but for me, the smell of fresh air and cool wind was something I always craved. Just after you were born, I didn't have much free time but the little I did, I spent taking solitary hikes and exploring nature.

One day, on the suggestion of a respected wildlife publication, I ventured to a seldom-visited area that was referred to as Echo Bridge. A massive passage that had been constructed hundreds of years ago and remained still surrounded by trees and wildlife. The reason for its erection was a great unknown; no one knew who built it or, more importantly, why a seemingly unnecessary bridge had been constructed in the middle of an unfrequented mass of forest.

The hike itself was particularly difficult. Reaching the location took a few hours and required a skilled eye to return safely. Looking back, it seems silly, but I had to know if what the article claimed was true... They wrote that the name Echo Bridge was quite literal and derived from the fact that if one stood directly beneath the structure and yelled, their voice would echo twenty times over. Yes, that was my idea of fun at the time.

After the advanced trek, I located it and stood in awe; the towering stone was something to marvel at and had almost a medieval quality to it. I climbed down and quickly assumed position below one end of the arch and yelled the word I believe most anyone would before trying to hear their voice echo: "Hello!" That single word was everything; my defining moment and deepest regret, my salvation, and demise.

As anyone in my position would figure, the greeting was intended to be rhetorical. I wasn't speaking or saying hello to anyone in particular. I heard my weary echo travel about twenty times over. Then suddenly, to my astonishment, something answered me back...

"Yes?" a cutting and shrill voice asked. I stood speechless, not sure if I'd heard something in the woods or in my own head. Either way, it couldn't be a voice. Then it spoke again, "What do you seek here? Do you seek heaven?"

I still wasn't sure how I should respond. It felt crazy, the situation was so unnatural. I don't know why but when I finally replied I said, "Yes." Looking back, I suppose it was the logical response to a yes or no question, but in hindsight, it was the wrong answer. I should have been asking the questions not answering them, but at the time, I had no reference to the breed of malevolence I was dabbling in.

"You must know hell to see the light, will you see both or neither?" What a spectacular question. If you got a chance to see one, but you had to see the other, is that a chance you take? Who even knew what the voice was speaking about? I was fascinated and star-struck; I'd been afforded an opportunity to communicate with something otherworldly.

That was the last time I remember feeling like I was in control of the path I followed. Once I gave my answer, everything changed forever. I never found a way to turn it off, a way to go back.

As I replied, "Yes," suddenly, I was taken. I left the forest in a flash, thrust to unimaginable heights; a million times that of the tallest roller-coaster. I entered through gaping holes of dripping blackness rimmed with hundreds of hobnailed tentacles. They massaged me as my anguish was one with my pleasure. The voice was now in my mind along with millions of others.

It's impossible to understand or picture but I was having millions of individual conversations at once. An evidence dump of galactic proportions that shouldn't have been digestible but somehow, I understood it. I understood it all. The paths fleshed out literally in the form of a planet-size bloodshot eyeball. Each of the sore, strained cracks was another parallel perspective; some the wickedest and most scarring of outcomes, some of inconceivable magnificence.

I eventually gathered, as I was ripped apart by the sides, deconstructed and reconstructed millions of times, that each was worth the other. In so many ways, they were actually identical. The voices brought me down every possible path of my reality, every crooked-rose vein on the weird cornea led to the same red lake. The gore pool on the far side of the all-seeing spectrum was where I could see the flailing optic nerve reach away from it all. The nasty niche of inclusivity where it all came to a point.

What should have felt like maddening whispers, showed me the truth: the world I was living in was impossible; a convincing temporary lie. The octopus and his cohorts had explained it to me thoroughly; it didn't matter if I destroyed the lives of those around me in one particular route because it still led to the equivalent finality of the path where I'd gone to church every day. The same people were all still there in the end. They were all standing, just waiting for me, and their arms were open as wide as the equator.

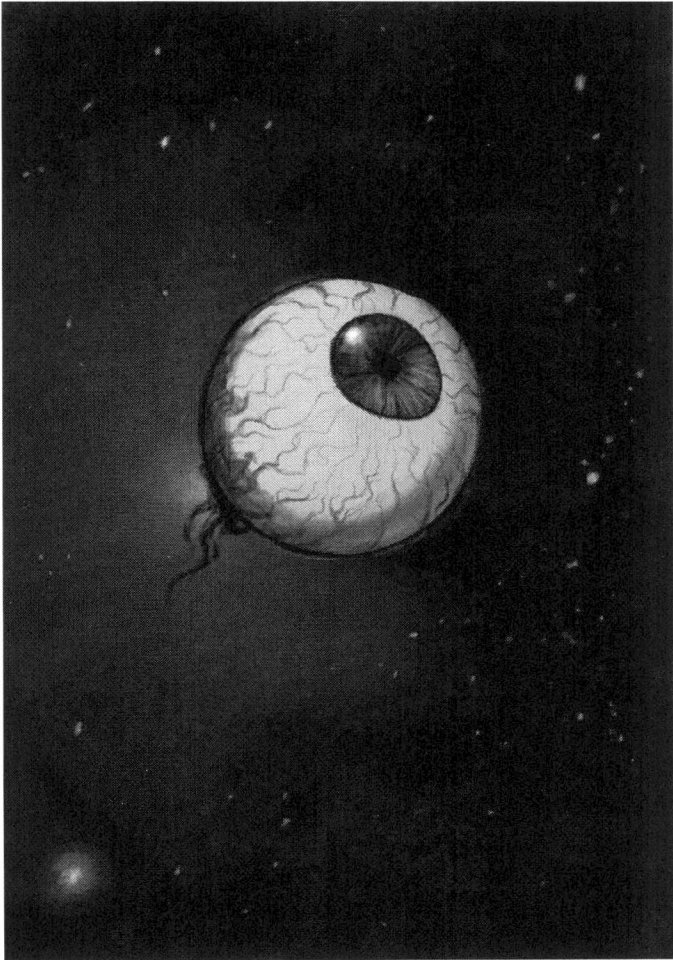

Everyone was there. In fact, it was more than everyone—it was innumerable versions of you, your father, my parents, our friends, everyone. There were versions of my parents that had chosen other partners to be with, which of course created versions of myself spliced with the DNA of the other suitors they'd selected. Bizarre manly and even more beautiful forms of myself stared me down, but they were void of any malice, they were all overjoyed to see me. There were millions of us, at least one for each that had been stored inside my skull.

Even stranger than all the other versions was the presence of the despicable, most sinister people I'd come to know. They stuck out like a sore thumb into the never-ending ocean of humanity. The sinners, the thieves, the bullies, the selfish, the criminals, and deviants. Those that could be associated with the most heinous acts pushed in-between us and integrated.

Then, suddenly, these evil people I'd crossed paths with, supposed scum as I saw them, felt just as cherished and necessary as the ones who treated me well. They were no longer a threat; they were just different. For just as the veins indicated, we're all exactly the same—we all are a singular algorithm.

The gory surface crater that we had met at the rear of the eye was deceptive. Once everyone had arrived, we realized it was actually a static meat-grinder of death. It fired up; the teeth of violence in all their yellowed neon glory began spinning. The spiked whips tore through us and took the army of bodies apart only to bring us closer together. The flesh of my flesh and blood of my blood spiraled sadistically until it pureed into a collective glob of everyone and everything. That is how I believe all of the voices came to be one. I witnessed the limits of reality explode like fireworks and dissipate before fading into the blackness.

We were all at peace, the full capacity of our consciousness transferred in thought and feeling. One colossal sphere of moving yin and yang, the equilibrium of darkness and light yielding and joining to form the gray that we were most familiar with.

The relief I felt was profound. I sensed the crushing weight that was life and all of its pressures lifted like I had been cured of the incurable. We were an all-encompassing spider web of togetherness, one that felt unbreakable. Our past actions meant nothing; all that mattered is what we were. I had finally found where I, no, where *we* needed to be. We had no reason to go anywhere, we were already home. In my heart, I knew we would be together forever, absolved of all curiosity. Until we weren't…

We all saw it as one; the multi-mouthed horned goliath let out a jarring screech. His hairy legs and razor hooves stomped in a mad frenzy. His mischievous leer mutated; he projected the solid representation of the united hells I had already swallowed to reach my Zen. I remember it quite clearly; his sharp, prickly fingers stunk of sewage and death as he pulled us apart. He ripped away chunks of us and ground them between the teeth of his many mouths; torturously, he sifted us apart. The fractures in our bliss were the worst pain I'd ever felt, and that was the last I saw of the nefarious creature.

I went tumbling back into the woods, under the bridge just as I was before. I found myself scrambling about confused in the foliage while my new abusers' disbelief and depression began to batter me. I couldn't be back—I didn't want to be. As much as I loved you and your father, I had already found you both and all else that I could have hoped to. HOW COULD I GO BACK?

I'd just unlocked myself and everyone else. The degree of this otherworldly enlightenment made the concept of assimilating back into society seem absurd. I sat overwhelmed and crying as darkness fell over the pitch-black forest. I had no idea how much time had lapsed; my journey had felt like an eternity.

"Why?!" I roared into the night skyline as my spinetingling echo reverberated again.

Back came the corrupt voice which had shown me the world. "Because you were curious, that's why. It's always the same reason, be it for you or anyone else whom has fielded my proposition."

"I wouldn't have wanted to see that if I had known! How do I get back?! I need it now, damn you! You know I need it!" My screams bore a half-truth, knowing what the world really was seemed to have ruined mine, or at least, significantly devalued it. Ignorance is bliss never seemed more applicable since there was no way to unsee it.

"No need to scream. Now that you've discovered me, speak in your mind and I shall hear you."

I followed its directions and heard my words again begging for the answer, and its retort was voiced loud and clear.

"It's not a matter of choice, you will go back, that is all you can do. If you die in these woods, you will never understand how to return. Death does not promise you reentry."

"Why are you speaking in riddles?! Just tell me what I must do to land there!"

"There are no words that will help you understand,

you must discover the answer yourself, then you will know. You shall find your way in this world again, but should you wish to go back and revel in eventuality, I will ask a favor of you. Each time once you've returned from scavenging for the answer, you must complete a task on my behalf, otherwise, your blindness shall not be lifted ever again."

I was then swept up from beneath the otherworldly bridge (or portal is how I tend to look at it) in the woods, and the next thing I recalled was having dinner with you and your father. I was nodding my head and listening to how your days went, the days that were now glaringly pointless.

I acted like I cared but I didn't; all I cared about was going back. The truth was the ultimate drug; once you'd had it, you yearned for it in fiendish fashion. Both your mind and body ached every moment with an undying eagerness. I was absolutely shattered.

The first question that came to my mind was had anyone else found this place? I had stumbled upon it randomly, but it quickly dawned on me that even if someone else had found it, there was no reason to talk about it. Why would I need to explain the bridge to any individual? To have the capacity to comprehend the explanation, it was essential to have the experience.

I wasn't concerned with unpacking or convincing people that I'd found the answer to the meaning of human existence. I knew that if I achieved the answer for myself, I achieved it for everyone. We would all come apart and come together again in the end. *Why* was a complex query I needed to eventually answer, but learning how to permanently dock was my top priority.

The idea that my reality no longer mattered helped make the decision easier to go back. Imagine being offered the keys to a door that obliterated everything you believed in, then imagine you could go back just by thinking about it. While I wondered what favors the strange voice from the woods might call upon me for, I had definitive, soul-shaking evidence that validated any action it could potentially ask of me would be just another exercise in the inane.

When the horror of the deeds I'd be required to commit came to light, I felt fine about it. I had already seen it, the actions I took throughout my path lead to the same destination. It sounded mad, so I had to keep continuously reminding myself but every time I did, I felt good about it. I could be a saint or serial killer, the present space (and those who occupied it) had become less relevant than ever.

I did ponder how I could keep searching if I was doing these awful things for the voice. The authorities of this reality would surely lock me away and toss out the key. I became concerned that my journey could be stunted swiftly and asked the voice, "What will become of me when the authorities of this world come to know what I've done?"

"The authorities of your world are just that, they shall not interfere with my wishes." I believed the voice with confidence, what choice did I have? I knew the concept was dangerous, it gave me purpose and it made me important, but that's not why I believed. I believed because I had been enlightened. I had seen and heard everything; I had become the universe.

Wondering what came next began to consume me. It didn't take long for me to call out to the voice again and beg to return me back to revelation. As I stared at the ceiling the next evening in my bed, I slowly began to prepare myself.

I felt the same warmth and agony as the first trip, it reconfirmed everything I experienced the first time. I paid very close attention and opened my receptors, expounding weighty concentration. While the hunt was intense and useful, I still couldn't find the answer and so that became my life; one relentless, grueling hunt.

I know now you would probably expect an apology, I recall what it was like to be in your shoes but I can no longer identify with it. The "Things" I did at the behest of that voice in the woods are horrific, at one time I would have believed that. Certainly, putting you in a chemical bath as a baby and telling you that you'd been born with a birth defect should enrage you. If not that, then explaining that I dismembered your father in cold blood and left you to believe you were a bastard should conjure a fierce ill will toward me. I know even some of the less personal acts in my box of things could very well make you have hatred for me.

But now, in context, after being educated and knowing what you know, you should grasp that any apology is purposeless. I understand the fantastic nature of what I'm telling you. I understand that this is not a story that can just easily be accepted at face value, but the proof lies in my acts. Ask yourself, how could I do so many awful things without repercussions? How could I mangle and take lives indiscriminately and live beside you quietly for your entire life? The answer is, I was being protected.

I spent decades in "the middle" as I called it, searching for the answers. The answers for you and the answers for everyone. These acts and my quest have drained me. My hunger for the answer has dwindled with age, each time I went back, I feel like I learned more but never enough. There are times when I've questioned it myself, times I've wondered if the voice has just been dangling a golden carrot and keeping me in a constant state of pursuit.

I took my last voyage yesterday. I decided it would be my last voyage when I returned. I still hadn't found it and I was feeling more tired than ever. Then the voice asked its favor, it commanded me to push you in front of a bus. Years ago, I would have done it without a second thought but I've lost my impulse, not my justification by my drive, and so I spared you. I spared you and instead will give myself.

Now you have to decide what you will do next. My hope is that you will continue my crusade. That you will go to Echo Bridge and call out to the voice and see if you can finish what I've started. Maybe I wasn't strong enough, maybe it is you who is meant to find the answer.

If you can find it then we all will find it and only then my death will not be in vain. Remember, Miles, all the people who avoided you and never even had the decency to meet your eyes don't matter. I beg that you find your way to the middle one day and learn that for yourself.

With Love Always,
Mom

Miles didn't know what to think of his mother's ravings. Had she really done these awful things and gotten away with it? She had either been touched by something unhuman or lost her mind. If she was the lunatic that she was portraying in her writing, then he would have at least seen a hint of it over time. He'd spent every evening with her after work thinking she'd been watching reruns. She was quite the actor, keeping hidden for so long.

The notion that nothing mattered was a sexy idea to him since he had nothing in his life and no one to enjoy it with any longer. It was still hard to fathom that good and evil weren't both independent of each other, that everything was a part of the same molecule and that his actions, be them disgraceful, charming, unacceptable, or otherwise, all landed the same result. Did the people who had outcast him deserve to feel hurt? Could the pursuit fill his emptiness and unite him with all he was missing?

He sat down with the box in one of the pair of rocking chairs in the living room, his mother typically occupied the other. On the last page of his mother's lengthy handwritten note was an old weathered article that looked like it had been trimmed from an outdoor magazine. It outlined directions that would supposedly bring the reader to a place called Echo Bridge, where if you called out, you could hear your voice repeat over and over. It made the destination seem like a charming little hike with a nice reward tucked away at the end.

He looked at the door only a few feet away and then back to the box. His purple forehead wrinkled; he didn't feel so awful anymore. He dipped his fingers back into the box and toyed around with the many papers inside. He concentrated and closed his eyes, trying to decide if the box was half empty or half full.

THE WOMAN ONCE AGAIN KNOWN AS PLAIN JANE

Plain Jane couldn't bear to look at herself in the mirror any longer. What she saw reflect back was repulsive; she had no curves, no color, and no charisma. Her medium physique was comprised of the worst of both worlds. She was only fat in some places, the ones that potential suitors wouldn't particularly appreciate. A gut that stuck out further than her breasts, sat above a flat backside and scrawny legs. It was as if she'd been created intentionally disproportionate. The numbing regularity of her situation was a pebble that would always be in her shoe, nagging with each step.

She sat down on the couch and turned on the television, exhausted with being so dreadfully normal. No one noticed if she arrived, no one noticed if she had left, people often had difficulty remembering her name. "Plain Jane" wasn't that hard to remember, was it? Being alone was the most depressing condition of her existence but what could she do? She just wasn't interesting and as far as she knew, there was no cure for a disease of that nature.

Why do I have to be so overlooked? Why have I been cursed? Why am I so painfully ordinary? How do I change it?! The questions repeated themselves relentlessly.

Living in Hollywood didn't help her chances either. In a city overflowing with glamorous gals and guys, and so much astonishing history, she was a microscopic fish in an ocean without a floor. As the thoughts pounded in Plain Jane's head, her beloved soap opera "The World Is Ours" was returning from commercial.

She held her breath as her favorite star, Francesca Abernathy, came into frame. The top-selling pop singer turned small-screen sensation serenaded the audience with her heavenly voice, performing the show's theme song as the opening credits rolled. Her beauty was incredible, Plane Jane sat in awe of her shining blonde hair, perfectly-rounded bosoms, and the striking smile that seduced every other man or woman she met.

If only there were a way for her to be like Francesca. If only somehow, with the snap of her fingers, Plain Jane could make people want to look at her and talk to her and fall in love with her like the TV goddess.

What happened next was unexpected. Usually, no one ever responded to the questions in Plain Jane's head, but the timing seemed too prophetic to be a coincidence. She didn't know if it was *the* answer but it was certainly *an* answer. One that was so loud that it was practically about to slap her in the face.

As Francesca finished hypnotizing her romantic interest on the screen, she locked lips with a muscular man and the program went to commercial. Without warning, a well-dressed and highly educated doctor looked through the tube at her like she was sitting across from him in the office at that precise moment.

"Tired of being Plain Jane in tinsel town? Are you sick of your talents being overlooked? Dr. Blade can fix all that. I can cut you open for an unreasonable rate. I can slice and carve you into a masterpiece. With experience in both medical science and being a professional sculptor, your future will know no bounds. Let me give you a stunning face for the red carpet... Or I can extract that nasty fat under your skin. Let me put my knife inside you, I guarantee one-of-a-kind, artistic results that will take you to the next level. Call 1-800-DR-BLADE now for a free consultation!"

It was a sign. Finally, she knew what was next; the good doctor had reached out and spoken directly to her. Dr. Blade would cut her open, remove the plain meat and fat, and load her full of extraordinary filler. The way Dr. Blade was talking, it sounded like it would be no sweat to make her look exactly like her idol, Francesca Abernathy! After that, when she walked into a room, they would bow at her feet and kiss them. No one would be able to forget her again.

But Plain Jane was confused, plastic surgery costs money and Dr. Blade, honest as he was, openly admitted his rates were downright unreasonable smack in the middle of his advertisement. She didn't even have enough for a weekend vacation at a roach motel, never mind the stiff fee she assumed Dr. Blade might require to cut her open. Then, suddenly, it struck her; she'd been given a sign. Her first question had been answered, she simply needed to ask the next question.

How will I get the money for Dr. Blade?

As the echoing words of the question reverberated in her head, the television projected the next answer immediately. A sharp-looking fellow in a navy-blue three-piece suit looked at her pointing a revolver, "Now you've got to ask yourself one question. Do I feel lucky? Well, do ya, punk?" As he pulled the trigger, a long cloth flag displayed below the barrel that read: ONLY $1!

The man began to laugh light-heartedly and dance about and his stone-serious demeanor evaporated. "Cause if you're feeling lucky, then why not try the new scratch ticket Luck of the Draw? For only a buck, with a one in five chance to win on every ticket, you could be swimming in green before you know it! What have you got to lose… Besides everything you hate, that is?"

There it was, all Plain Jane would need to do now was go down to the liquor store and buy a Luck of the Draw scratch ticket. Then she would have the money to pay for the alterations that would give her a nice life. She would be a somebody in no time at all, she thought, swiftly grabbing hold of her pocketbook and long coat.

She rushed down to the liquor store and was faced with a man she saw often; a fat slob that paid her no attention no matter how many times she'd come inside the establishment. She advanced toward the cluttered counter and looked him dead in the eye, "May I have one Luck of the Draw ticket, please?" Plain Jane asked.

The fat slob kept reading his newspaper, despite being in listening range. He couldn't be bothered.

She repeated herself a little louder and once again, received nothing in return. Finally, she reached out and touched his sausage-like fingers, reiterating her inquiry for the third time. This attempt successfully elicited a response.

"That's a very popular game. We sold all the tickets already, lady. In fact, I just sold the last one to that guy over there," he said, pointing to a boring-looking man standing by the magazine rack.

Plain Jane was shocked. When she entered the store initially, she thought the fat slob was the only other person inside. She had looked around but didn't notice anyone else. The boring man might have been standing near the magazine rack but he wasn't reading anything. Instead, he was staring directly at her as if he'd been waiting. A frightening smirk cut into his expression, a disturbing constant.

Plain Jane tossed all of her alarm and apprehension aside and strode toward the man at once. "Excuse me, sir? I couldn't help but notice you've been staring at me and that fat slob just informed me that you purchased the last Luck of the Draw ticket, is that true?"

"Yes, I've been staring at you and yes, I absolutely purchased the final ticket," he replied somberly.

"Well, you see, I was supposed to buy that last ticket. No one notices me and—"

"I noticed you," said the boring man, interrupting.

She paused momentarily before ignoring his statement altogether, "The reality is I haven't been well at all. I haven't been well for a long time, not since I can remember anyway. But I've found a path today. This ticket will give me the money for Dr. Blade to cut me open and his incisions will make me well again."

"I can put my blade inside you for free, I know how to cut someone open too. Then you wouldn't even need my ticket."

"Yes, but are you an artist? Dr. Blade is not only a surgeon, he's a sculptor. If I can be frank, you don't strike me as the artistic type."

"No, you're right, I'm no artist. I don't do a lot that's exciting."

"Then may I pay you for the ticket?"

"Why would I sell you a ticket you are telling me is worth many thousands of dollars? What if, even though you're not well, you're somehow right? Then I would be a total fool, wouldn't I?"

"Maybe there is something I can give you that's worth more to you than money."

"Like what?"

"Will you come into the alley with me?"

The boring man gave no response but followed Plain Jane out of the store and into the alley. It had started raining and the smell of the soaked, rancid garbage made for a strange romantic atmosphere. Plain Jane got on her knees and unzipped the boring man's trousers.

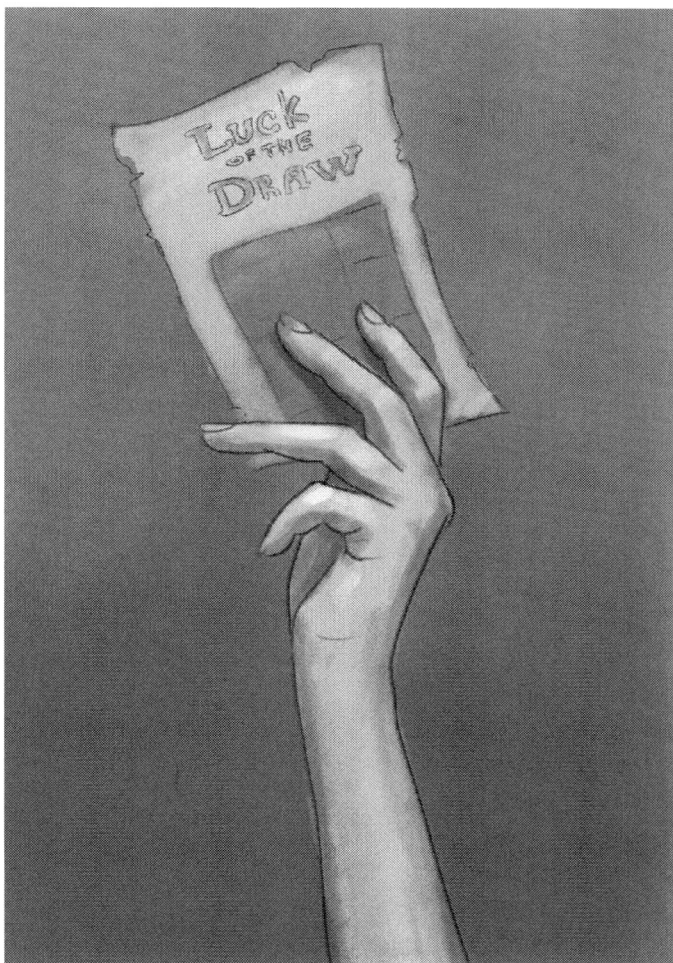

He smelled of mothballs, pistachio, and aged leather. She took him entirely inside her throat and in between swallows, she made him promises. She told him that once Dr. Blade made her beautiful that she would come back to him and he could have her whenever he liked.

The boring man never found climax but eventually, she tugged the ticket away from his waxy grip. Plain Jane then stood up unfolding her now-bloody knees and pulled the chunks of pebbles and broken glass from her oozing skin. "Can't wait to reopen the scabs for you once I'm beautiful," she promised, staring into the boring man's emotionless face.

He walked away from her without saying another word. Within a matter of seconds, Plain Jane had fished a penny from her pocketbook and was scraping at the moist scratch ticket like a gambling addict. It took her only a few minutes to reveal all of the silver spaces, but everything had all played out just as she'd suspected; she was officially filthy rich.

***

After collecting her winnings, Plain Jane scheduled and completed surgery the same day with Dr. Blade. In spite of his unreasonable rates, she still had plenty of money left over to play with. She was so excited about the transformation that she asked Dr. Blade not to put her under for the operation. She grinned with ecstasy as her body went numb and the serrated metal stabbed wildly into her. With each back and forth, she felt him cutting away all of the average—piles and piles of it—until the weight of normalcy had at last been trimmed from her vessel entirely.

It had taken a few weeks to heal but the drugs Dr. Blade gave Plain Jane had sped up her recovery tremendously. When she removed her bandages, she marveled at her fresh perfection; she had become the living embodiment of Francesca Abernathy. The doctor was good on his word and just as he'd promised, he molded her with a clone-worthy exactness. She WAS the trim yet busty drop-dead gorgeous superstar.

She looked into the body-length mirror in awe; a feeling she didn't think was possible before. The repulsive misshapen fat was nowhere to be found; she now wore her hero's Barbie Doll dimensions. The enormous fake tits would take some getting used to, they felt a bit different then she'd anticipated. The swimming fun bags added some stress to her lower back but were visually picture-perfect.

Her face was by far the new feature she coveted the most, mainly because it wasn't hers. Plain Jane's nose was whittled down to a triangular shape and her cheeks were now sharp and flat. She puckered her plump-to-capacity lips and thought about how much more fun it would be to fuck herself now.

The one standout of her makeover was the scabs on her knees. Despite the vast majority of her body's scars having healed seamlessly, her knees remained raw and bloody. *That fucking bastard*, she thought, recalling the deal she had made with the boring man in the alley.

She didn't truly mean it. Just as her scars had vanished, so did any intent behind the promise she'd made to that boring bastard. She knew right as he walked away that day, while she'd assured him access to and reciprocation from her new beautiful body, that there was no way in hell she would be returning back to him. It had always been an empty promise but one that she needed to make, otherwise the boring man could have encumbered her fate.

Besides, there were too many other men who weren't so dreadfully boring to focus on. The attention she was receiving from everyone now was astounding.

She was no longer going by Plain Jane anymore. Dr. Blade's work was so good that she was able to call herself Francesca Abernathy now and no one was the wiser. The finished product was so convincing that she began to be hounded for autographs and photos (which she always declined).

Each of these innumerable everyday interactions gave her a shot of adrenaline and that was just from the scumbag low-lifers around her. Drunk off the constant recognition, she pondered her next steps; *how could this amazing new addiction evolve?* The answer was more forthcoming than she thought. It was lying in wait at the one place she used to hate, the one place that she couldn't bear to look before—the mirror.

She was Francesca Abernathy, but reality wouldn't permit two of the same being to exist in parallel. If she wanted to equal that fame and prestige of her doppelgänger, there was only one way she knew of. She decided then that she should kill Francesca Abernathy. Her new vehicle would allow her to discreetly take her place. Once the grim task was complete, it would be her on the television and singing songs. It would be her sitting inside the Hollywood mansion hosting bashes.

The plan within her mind felt humble enough. She would simply go to her house, stab her, cut her into pieces, and dispose of her in one of the nearby manhole caps. Surely, the rats would make use of her bleeding meat.

Just before bed, she picked out the biggest knife from her kitchen and slashed at the darkness in front of her. That was enough practice to satisfy her, she didn't want to overexert herself. She needed rest for the next evening she would venture off to dismember the outdated version of Francesca Abernathy.

***

The woman formerly known as Plain Jane left her house on foot. It took hours before she reached the neighborhood where Francesca Abernathy resided. She lurked in the tall bushes outside her residence dressed in a style that closely emulated the popular celebrity. She watched the guard at the front gate and monitored the whole neighborhood suspiciously. She kept quiet as she waited for her opportunity until she heard a voice behind her…

"Oh, my God! Francesca Abernathy! I'm your biggest fan!"

The woman formerly known as Plain Jane turned around to meet a familiar face, a likeness she thought she would never see again; that of the boring man. What an odd coincidence! Based on his enthusiasm, he seemed to be a big fan. He was more excited about their current encounter than when he was lodged in her former throat back in the alley.

"Please keep quiet!" she commanded with a muffled urgency.

"I love side B of your fourteenth record, Mad House, and you're always wonderful on The World Is Ours. I just can't believe it's you!"

"Can't believe it's me? Can't you? I mean, you're standing right outside my fucking mansion, aren't you?!"

The boring man was testing her patience. She had come to slash Francesca Abernathy to ribbons, not to be put to sleep by the boring man's redundant banter.

"Oh, this is your house? I had no earthly idea…"

"Very funny, but I'm afraid everyone knows that I live here. It sounds like you're being facetious. Are you being facetious, sir?"

"No, hardly, I was actually here for other reasons but it seems rather odd that you would be standing outside of your house looking in, don't you think?"

His question caught her off guard a moment before she rebounded, "I have to be sure that the gate workers are doing their job. You know good help is hard to find these days."

"Yes, this is true. In fact, some weeks ago, I myself made an agreement with a woman. I helped her tremendously and she offered to help me in return, although sadly once my end of the bargain was complete, she stopped helping me. So, you see, I understand exactly what you mean really."

The woman, formerly known as Plain Jane, turned around a bit flustered by the boring man's whining. He seemed upset with her but he couldn't possibly know who she really was. "That sounds like quite the raw deal for you," she replied dismally.

"The reason I assumed it wasn't your house was that I noticed you've been living in the city as of late. I mean you walked here, didn't you?"

"You've been following me?! How—how dare you! You scoundrel!"

The boring man removed a hammer from the inside of his jacket and played with it, feeling the weight in his hand. "That may be true, but I haven't forgotten that you have something that's owed to me."

The dirty steel cracked against the side of her head, caving part of the rounded area in. Before the red soaked into her artificial, bleach-blonde locks completely, the boring man threw her in the trunk of his car.

***

When the woman formerly known as Plain Jane awoke, she was in a dark room with a blinding light pointed directly at her. She couldn't move or speak and her throat was dry and irritated.

"Oh, finally, up are we? Praise the Lord, I was getting worried there for a minute. I thought you might never come to."

The light switch flipped, illuminating the entire room a few seconds later. A massive circular mirror sat fixed to the ceiling above her. Her worst nightmare had come to light; she no longer had the features that fate had brought her to acquire.

Her radically modified body (or what was left of it) was glued to a filthy cement slab, surrounded by a pool of shadow. She had been left isolated on an island of agony. Her feeble squirms did no good as the alterations had left her immobilized; she had become the shell of supremacy.

Her hair had been dyed back to the same shitty brown that she was born with, her breasts had been cut down considerably, and her flawlessly-molded face had been broken and distorted. Instead of being the result of Dr. Blade's masterpiece, she looked like a mistake. The same mistake she was when she first met the boring bastard.

On top of her reconstruction, he had taken all of her limbs, her legs from the shin down, and her arms from just above the elbow; they weren't bleeding anymore but they were missing. The wounds had been tidily stitched and the disjointed parts were hung up on the wall behind her. It all seemed very well organized.

The waters of misery and ire drifted down her face uncontrollably, the boring man had severed her extremities and aspirations. She cursed him but the grimy rag in her mouth made any speech inaudible.

"That person you were becoming wasn't you. You wanted it to be, but it wasn't." He took a few steps closer to her twitching raw stumps.

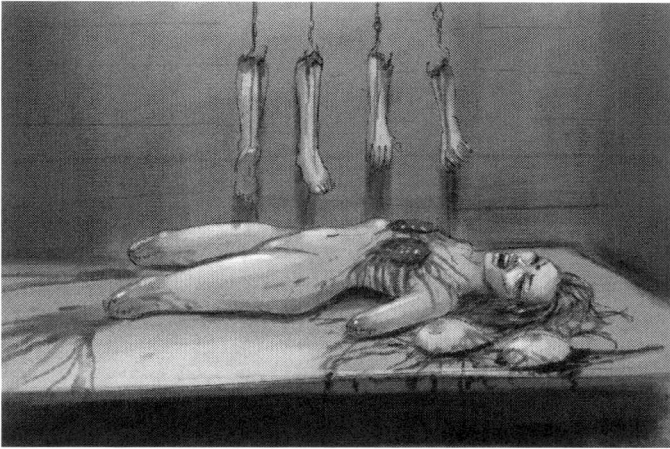

"You don't have to hide anymore under someone else's skin, you don't have to worry. You never thought anyone was paying attention, but I paid out so much that it left me broke. I always cared; I just never could quite figure out a way to tell you. At the same time, I wanted you to be happy, but you took it too far. You perverted yourself. You took it to a point where I could tell that you could no longer remember what joy was. So, I needed to show you again. The only question I have left to ask you is, do you remember now? Do you remember what it's like to be happy?"

The woman, once again known as Plain Jane, lethargically nodded her head, for the bloody infused tears streaming down were no longer tears of sadness––they were tears of joy.

ABOUT THE AUTHOR

I will keep writing disturbing and strange stories. I will keep writing sick crime stories with a thick pulpy goodness that's so girthy you might find it in your fucking orange juice (if you drink the one with pulp included). I will continue to leverage my life experience (good times and bad, happy and sad) to amuse you however I'm able to. I write for myself, but for those who dig this sort of shit, I want to do the right thing for you. If I can put a grimace on your face, or take you away from your problems and give you someone else's for a day or two, that would give me a great sense of purpose. I wish I could do this full time, maybe some day that will be possible.
Maybe with your help. You sick fuck.

WHEN THEY SAW HIS FACE, THEY WISHED IT WAS A MASK...

What do a brilliant child killer, a hopeful special effects artist, a duo of budding teen spree killers, a student-screwing teacher, and a mutated maniac with his lower jaw missing have in common?

They're all out this Halloween.

How will their paths cross? Who will be butchered? Can anyone survive this bloodbath or are they all destined to drown in a pool of warm red? This slasher nightmare gives you a seat right beside the killer but don't get too comfortable, there's a Scary Bastard on the loose...

ORIGINAL, HAND-DRAWN HIDEOUS WORKS OF ART INCLUDED

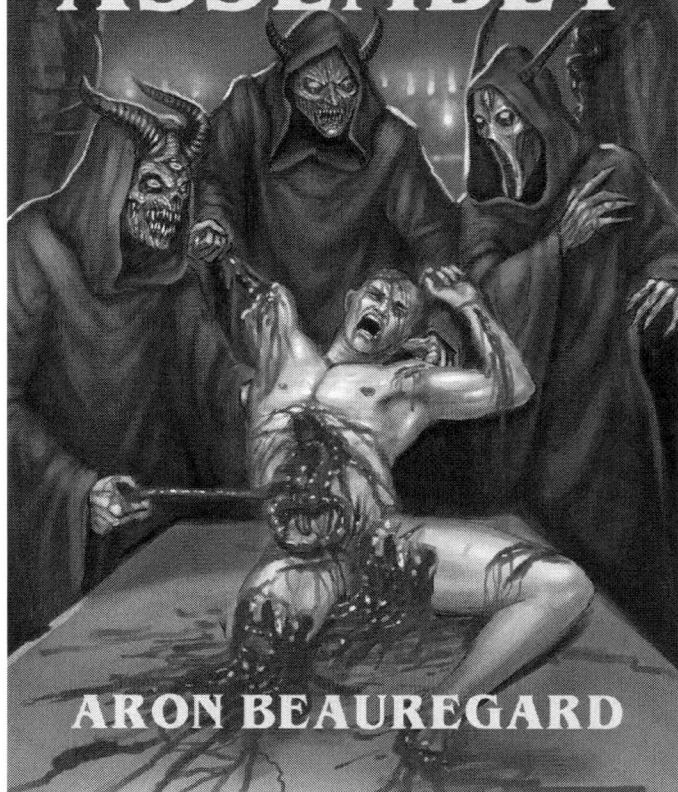

DARK
ASSEMBLY

ARON BEAUREGARD

TAKE PRIDE IN YOUR DYSFUNCTION

This assembly of putrid tales will drag you into the darkest regions of humanity. It will push extremes and test the mental moral boundaries of those who choose to participate. Meet a woman who carries a dead baby in her womb that she believes will somehow find life again. Join two teenage psychopaths as they bring hell to the suburbs on Devil's Night. Follow a child of the streets that finally steered away from a life of crime, only to be drawn back by a bizarre new drug. Take part in a gruesome and nefarious ritual that can restore one's innocence, or worm your way into the dark web beside a sadistic pedophile with a bottomless desire to kill and fuck.

How should you feel after digesting these admittedly obscene and repulsive stories? Ask yourself if enjoying them makes you a horrible person or if hating them somehow justifies your journey into this storm of violence and perversion. For the sick and willing, please join in our Dark Assembly...

INCLUDES REPULSIVE, HAND-DRAWN ABOMINATIONS

SECRET TRIP ART

The three characters from "Making Room in the Birdhouse" crucified in the next version of hell they would find...

Printed in Great Britain
by Amazon